"I'm going to ravish every inch of you," Caleb whispered in the total darkness

Her voice trembled with need. "Please…"

"I'll take you right here, right now. Up against the wall. Hard and fast. It's dark. You can't even see my face. You couldn't even describe me to the authorities."

"But I've been a very bad girl." Her playful tone let him know she was enjoying their game. "I've told the police where they can find you."

Caleb sank to his knees. "I'm going to have to give you a tongue-lashing." He spanned both hands at the curve of her waist and slowly trailed his tongue from her breasts to her navel. Stroking her hip, he discovered she still wore thong panties and thigh-high stockings.

"You really are as mercurial as the wind. One minute coy, the next playful. Who are you really?" he urged.

"My identity is a secret, just as you're a complete mystery to me."

Hmm. Meggie liked subterfuge in the bedroom. And as long as he wore his mask and played Don Juan, he could provide her with everything. But what could he offer her as plain ordinary Caleb Greenleaf? The unsettling thought stilled his sexual hunger.

But not for long…

Dear Reader,

This is the last book in my BACHELORS OF BEAR CREEK miniseries. Writing a cross-line series for both Blaze and Duets has been quite challenging, and I can only hope all my hard work has paid off.

Meggie and Caleb's story was particularly poignant for me as I explored darker—and sexier!—themes than I've ever before explored. Both Meggie and Caleb take erotic risks that lead them on a sometimes chaotic, but always thrilling path to self-discovery.

As I wrote, I found myself asking tough questions of these "best-friends-turned-lovers." Questions that include the masks we wear both figuratively and literally when we're falling in love, the mind games we play with each other and the roles we choose to assume.

I've tried my very hardest to write a story that sizzles, but even more, I poured my heart and soul into these characters, reaching deep inside myself to create a real sense of romance, love and respect between my hero and heroine. Although I do hope you enjoy this red-hot read, I also hope you come away with a sharper sense of your own self and what risks are worth taking in the pursuit of true love!

Sincerely,

Lori Wilde

P.S. Don't forget to check out tryblaze.com!

Books by Lori Wilde

The Bachelors of Bear Creek

30—A TOUCH OF SILK (Blaze)
79—SEXY, SINGLE AND SEARCHING (Duets)
EAGER, ELIGIBLE AND ALASKAN (Duets)

HARLEQUIN DUETS

63—BYE, BYE BACHELORHOOD
COAXING CUPID
50B—I LOVE LACY

A THRILL TO REMEMBER

Lori Wilde

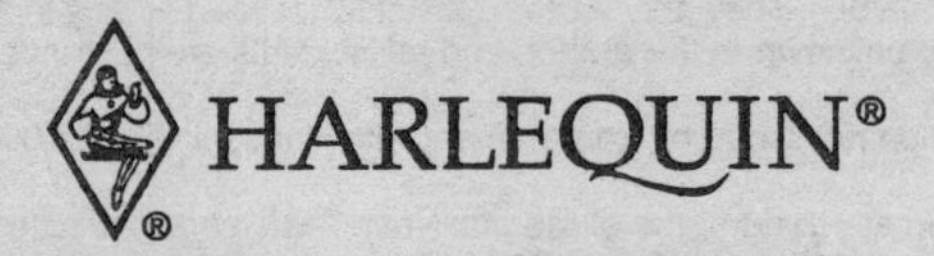

TORONTO • NEW YORK • LONDON
AMSTERDAM • PARIS • SYDNEY • HAMBURG
STOCKHOLM • ATHENS • TOKYO • MILAN • MADRID
PRAGUE • WARSAW • BUDAPEST • AUCKLAND

To Renee M. Roy—
you're a darned fine writer.
Keep at it. One day it will be your name
on the front of a book.

ISBN 0-373-79070-8

A THRILL TO REMEMBER

This edition published by arrangement with Harlequin Books S.A.

Visit us at www.eHarlequin.com

Printed in U.S.A.

1

WHO WAS THAT masked woman?

Spellbound, Caleb Greenleaf watched the auburn-haired lady in red strut through the front door of the Bear Creek, Alaska, community center and into the rowdy, masked costumed ball hosted by New York City's trendiest women's magazine, *Metropolitan.*

"Red, hot and rockin'" he muttered under his breath, narrowing his eyes and studying her more closely in the muted, atmospheric lighting.

Tall. Curvy in all the right places. Good legs.

Correction. Very, very good legs.

In fact, showcased so fetchingly in those four-inch, heartbreaker-red stilettos, they might even be the most stupendous pair of gams he'd ever clamped eyes upon.

The tight, scarlet bustier she wore snugged her luscious body like a second skin. The satiny material flared out provocatively over those generous curves before nipping in again at her narrow waist.

Below the bustier she had on crimson tap pants that barely covered her bodacious bottom. Then came vermilion fishnet stockings topped with a black lace garter that set his pulse charging like a stampeding bison. She was as vibrant as a Vegas showgirl and three times as sexy.

The term *brick house* permeated his brain.

He recognized the lingerie. Had seen similar attire at Dolly's House, a brothel museum in Ketchikan, gracing the voluptuous wax figure of Alaska's most notorious gold-rush madam, Klondike Kate.

What a costume.

What a body.

What a woman!

Who was she?

Brazenly, Caleb ogled, not the least bit ashamed of himself, which wasn't like him at all. No hound dog, he. In fact, he was leaning against the wall in the insouciant slouch he'd carefully perfected for unwanted social occasions such as this.

An introvert by nature, he found his job as a naturalist for the state of Alaska suited his personality. Caleb spent a great deal of his time alone, in the outdoors, and he treasured his freedom. He avoided big parties, but since he was one of the guests of honor, he couldn't steer clear of this shindig. Even though townspeople, husband-hungry wannabe brides, curious tourists and an assortment of media types packed the community center, he was suddenly very glad he had come.

Just inside the foyer, she hesitated. He observed her make the conscious decision to proceed in spite of her fear. She squared her shoulders, pasted a smile on her luscious lips and sallied forth. That split second of vulnerability, followed by her resolute marshaling of courage, touched him in an oddly tender way, and he almost applauded.

In she stalked. *Boom-shaka-boom-shaka-boom.* Her breasts bounced jauntily.

Wowza!

Watching her bottom sway caused Caleb's body to tighten, his temperature to spike and his breathing to quicken. A seething longing gripped his gut. In conjunction, the wistful flavor of yearning burned on his tongue. He wanted her. Badly.

She aroused him with the stunning impact of blunt force trauma. No woman had aroused him quite like this since the object of his very horny teenage fantasies—Meggie Scofield.

He grinned crookedly at that memory. At one time he'd been so infatuated with his best friend's sister Caleb had thought he would never get her out of his head. And unfortunately, Meggie, who was two years older, had never seen him as anything more than a surrogate kid brother. It had taken both a stint in college and his stepbrother Jesse marrying Meggie for him to let go of his youthful obsession.

As the last of the four Bear Creek Bachelors who had advertised for wives in *Metropolitan* magazine, Caleb had just about surrendered all hope of finding someone who inflamed him in the same way Meggie once had. But then, out of the clear azure sky, in marched sexy Klondike Kate, piquing his interest and stirring long dormant passions.

Was she a tourist? He knew everyone in town. She certainly wasn't a local. Maybe she was with the magazine.

He couldn't stop staring at her. She sashayed over to the bar, ordered a glass of wine and started chatting up the bartender. Lucky bastard.

Look at me, Caleb willed her. *Forget that joker and look at me.*

As if compelled by his silent entreaty, she raised her head and glanced across the room.

Their gazes clashed like lightning striking. Hot. Intense. Compelling.

Heavy-duty.

Her eyes widened behind the showy red-feathered mask that hid the upper portion of her face. She moistened her lips with the tip of her pink tongue and Caleb just about came undone. In an instant, his overactive imagination transported him to a world of his own making.

She's splayed spread-eagle across his big, king-size bed in that daring damned underwear.

"Come here," she invites.

He's out of his clothes and beside her quicker than you can melt butter in a microwave.

She kisses him with a vital pressure, thrusting her honeyed tongue against his. Heat rushes to his groin, whetting his voracious appetite.

He unhooks her bustier, allows it to fall open and expose her full, creamy breasts. When he growls low in his throat, she closes her eyes and softly coos, "Help yourself."

Bending his head, he takes one budded pink nipple into his warm mouth. She hisses drawing in a breath. Desire shoots through him. She encourages him to continue by holding his head in place.

"Harder," she whimpers. "Don't be gentle."

Reaching down, she runs her hand over the length of his shaft, greedily signaling to him exactly what she needs. Her fingers tangle with the leather strings on his pants and she gives a series of short firm jerks that send a shower of sparks scorching through his groin.

He is beside himself with cravings for this marvelous creature. He could take her right here, right now, with no thoughts except to quench his undying thirst for her. But he doesn't. He wants her to be as desperate for him as he is for her.

Hungrily, he cups her breasts together, filling his palms, so he can easily drift from one to the other with a quick flick of his tongue.

Her moans almost send him over the edge of reason, plunging him headfirst into a world of sensation of which he has only dreamed.

Pure heaven.

He feels himself grow stiffer, not even realizing such hardness was possible. His brain is addled by the sweet scent of her womanhood, the luxurious touch of her hair, the heavenly taste of her skin, the hypnotic sound of her voice.

More. He had to have more.

''Hey, guy.'' A lithesome brunette dressed as Elvira, Mistress of the Dark, sidled up to him and shattered his reverie.

''Yes,'' he replied rather curtly. *Gee thanks, lady, for interrupting the grandest fantasy I've had in years.*

''Ooh, the dark, brooding type. My favorite.'' She circled her index finger around the rim of her champagne glass and batted her eyelashes at him.

Aggressive women had approached him many times before. Especially after he'd made it rich and even more especially after the June issue of *Metropolitan* had hit the stands. All too well he recognized that flint-edged expression in her eyes, and he could almost hear the *cha-ching* sound of a cash register echoing in her head.

Gold digger, he diagnosed, right off the bat.

"So, who are you suppose to be?" Elvira purred.

"What?"

Her gaze roved over him. "Let me guess. Zorro?"

"No."

She snapped her fingers. "I know. You look like Johnny Depp in that movie *Don Juan Demarco.* You're supposed to be Don Juan, the infamous Latin lover."

"Uh-huh." Caleb nodded, barely glancing at the woman. He wished she'd go away and let him resume his fantasy.

"So say something sexy to me." She winked.

He frowned.

"Brooding and silent. Okay, then I'll say something sexy to you. I really love the way your leather pants fit, if you catch my drift."

Great. He was lusting after Klondike Kate but he'd gotten stuck with Miss Hot-for-Your-Wallet.

Undaunted by his lack of response, Elvira continued. "Somebody told me you're that millionaire bachelor. Is that true?"

"Sorry." He shook his head. "Don't have a penny to my name."

"Oh." Her eyes rounded in alarm as if she'd just stepped in a big pile of something unsavory with her expensive designer shoes.

And his friends claimed he was too cynical. Well, he had his reasons.

From the beginning of this whole advertising-for-wives venture, Caleb had been reluctant to join his friends. Not that he was afraid of commitment—he did yearn for the same intimacy and happiness the ad had generated for his three buddies, Quinn, Jake and Mack. But given his family's history of numerous weddings and divorces, stepfamilies merging and then dissolving, he was a bit leery of marrying for any reason other than true love.

You're paranoid, Greenleaf. Terrified of getting involved with a woman like your mother who ditches rich husbands for even richer ones. Or of winding up like your dad, down and out after two failed marriages.

Okay, all right. Perhaps he *was* sensitive on the subject. And maybe he did have trust issues when it came to women.

At age twenty-seven, he had amassed a small fortune by translating his love of the wilderness into a lucrative dot-com company that supplied indigenous flora and fauna to universities and laboratories. When he'd sold the company in the midst of the bull market and parlayed his hobby into a cool million, he'd discovered that other than impressing his hard-to-please, social-climbing mother, the money had been a hindrance rather than a boon.

He realized too late he shouldn't have worn the attention-grabbing Don Juan costume. He couldn't say why he'd chosen the guise of the infamous lothario. Perhaps because he was nothing like the gregarious Spanish lover and it was easier pretending to be something he wasn't. More than likely it was because the outfit had been fairly simple to put together.

But if he was honest with himself he would admit

the Don Juan masquerade *did* elicit a certain confidence in him. Something about these leather pants, shiny black boots, dashing cape, dapper fake mustache and billowy white pirate's shirt stoked his confidence in a way he couldn't explain. The costume served as a conduit for the darker side of his personality and dared him to act upon impulses he normally would have suppressed.

Like the urge to glide across the room and introduce himself to Klondike Kate.

He had never been one for casual sex, although in college he'd indulged in a few short-term flings in an attempt to douse his desire for Meggie. But the woman in red made him so darned hot that he was ready and willing and open for just about anything.

Short-term, long-term. He didn't care. He just wanted to get to know her.

And, after much speculation, he was ready to call off the wife search and plunge headlong into a reckless affair in order to ease his sexual frustration.

Tonight he was suave Don Juan.

Anything was possible.

Go on. Do it.

He searched for his crimson goddess, but she had walked away. He was bereft for a moment, but then he caught a flash of red as she disappeared into the costumed throng gyrating on the dance floor in time to a jivey disco version of ''Wild, Wild West.''

He exhaled.

''Wild, Wild West'' morphed into ''Super Freak.'' Blood strummed in his temples and his heart pounded like a headhunter's drum. Panic scratched through him at the thought she might leave the party before he could speak to her.

Where had she gone?

"Will you excuse me?" he asked Elvira, and before she could reply, he pushed off from the wall and went to prowl through the crowd.

After several minutes of searching, he spied Klondike Kate sitting alone in a cloth-backed chair positioned in a dimly lit alcove just off the main hall.

He smiled to himself.

Gotcha.

One high-heeled shoe dangled from her hand and she was slowly massaging her foot. At the sight of those delicate toes, painted not stark scarlet as he might have suspected, but a beguilingly innocent cotton-candy pink, Caleb's lodged in his throat. She inclined her head, exposing the gentle sloping curve of her neck, and he had to bite down hard on the inside of his cheek to keep from moaning out loud. His gut constricted, his muscles loosened, his body warmed—and extreme reaction he recognized but could not seem to control. His unexplained nervousness scared him, smacking of a weakness he did not want to accept.

Don't let her get to you.

It had simply been too long since he'd had sex. That was why he was so susceptible to her allure. No other reason.

Yeah, right. If mere horniness was what motivated him, then why not take advantage of the dozens of women who'd thrown themselves at him all summer?

Nope, this was different, even if he couldn't say why.

Klondike Kate started to lean forward to slip her shoe back on, but stopped short. His gaze tracked her movements. He noticed one of the hooks on her bustier had snagged the chair's tweed cloth.

Squirming, she tried unsuccessfully to dislodge herself.

This is your chance to meet her, Greenleaf. Don Juan to the rescue.

Heart thudding, he hurried over, boldly leaned down, pressed his mouth to her ear and heard himself whisper in a debonair Spanish accent that sounded nothing like his natural voice, "Please, allow me. It would be my greatest honor to assist you."

DON JUAN'S MANLY HANDS rested on her bare back, his fingers finessing the hook of her bustier.

Meggie Scofield caught her breath, stunned that the drop-dead gorgeous man in the black leather mask who had been staring so blatantly at her ever since she strolled into the community center was touching her in a most intimate fashion and causing a frisson of heat to spread fanlike over her tender flesh.

No. No. This was much too soon. The guy was more than she had bargained for. She wasn't ready for this much masculine attention.

It had taken every ounce of courage she possessed—plus generous encouragement from her friends and a hefty quaff of chardonnay—to stroll into the party wearing this skimpy outfit. If she hadn't been so darned determined to shed her goody-goody image she wouldn't have made it this far.

But now she was paralyzed, intoxicated by the smoldering nearness of this stranger. He stood so close his spicy cologne filled her nostrils with the bracing combination of orange zest, piquant cinnamon and rich licorice. He smelled like a holiday feast.

Anticipation, charged and fiery, crackled between them. Adrenaline shot through her veins, prickled her sensitive skin, seeped beneath the auburn wig she wore over her coal-black tresses.

Who was he? And why did he seem so fascinated with plain ordinary Meggie Scofield, when a man like him could have any available woman in the room?

It's the costume, ninny.

Disquieting heat waves shimmered through her body as his fingers tripped down her spine. She shivered and shifted away from him.

"Hold still," he murmured in a low Spanish accent so erotically seductive it caused the fine hairs at the nape of her neck to lift. "I fear sudden movement will render your beautiful garment worthless."

"Sorry."

"No reason to apologize."

Her heart hammered restlessly. His leather-clad hip was level with her shoulder. She dropped her gaze to his knee-length, shiny leather riding boots, and had to force herself not to shiver again.

For some reason she could not fathom, Meggie envisioned rubbing her fingers over the soft, fluid folds of his silky white shirt. The unexpected image sent goose bumps skittering up her arm, and the budded tips of her breasts stiffened against the lace of her bustier.

She gulped.

This whole moment felt weirdly surreal, as if she were moving in slow motion through a favorite recurring dream. When she was younger her secret fantasies had been chockful of ferociously naughty characters like Don Juan. Rock stars and motorcycle men. Pirates and Vikings and irascible black sheep. But those days were gone. She'd had her fill of rogues, and she was finished with living vicariously through risk-taking men.

She wanted her own adventures.

Except her body wasn't listening to her mind's vehement denial.

"There," he pronounced. "You are free."

Meggie leaped from the chair, almost careening into him in an urge to remove herself from his disconcerting proximity.

"Thank you," she murmured.

Unable to resist peeking, she shot him a sidelong glance. The intense blue eyes lurking behind his black leather mask rocked her, upsetting her equilibrium.

"You're most welcome."

He kept his voice low, and she wondered if the Spanish accent was real or if it was simply perfected for his Don Juan persona. She remembered then that she was supposed to be in character, too, and she should be speaking with the bawdy, teasing drawl of Klondike Kate. But bowled over by her body's unexpected response to this stranger, she couldn't force herself to speak above a whisper.

Whoever this guy might be in real life, in costume he was a dead ringer for the infamous Spaniard. Had he chosen his costume because he was indeed a masterful lover?

He caught her watching him, and Meggie's stomach fluttered. Deliberately, he raised a hand and slowly traced an index finger over his pencil thin mustache in a surprisingly intimate gesture.

Her gaze darted from his eyes to his mouth and back again and her chest squeezed.

Look away! Look away!

But she could not.

His audacious gaze collided head-on with hers. Smoldering, fervent, deeply blue. He possessed the sort of eyes to make any woman tremor with sexual anticipation. Eyes that promised a thousand taboo pleasures.

He didn't smile; his expression remained one of inexplicable containment. His lips were full; his jaw-line solidly masculine.

Who was he?

There was something incredibly powerful about the secrecy of his masquerade. Was the man beneath the mask just as potentially explosive as he appeared?

His masculine aura of supreme self-confidence seduced her, while at the same time made her extremely skittish. Her heart galloped and she did, indeed, tremble. Meggie hated the torturous, achy sensation and the helpless vulnerability that such potent physical attraction implied.

"You are cold."

Say something flip and flirty. Something Klondike Kate would say, the voice in the back of her head urged.

But overwhelmed by this man and her body's response to him, she couldn't find her tongue.

He whipped off the black cape from around his neck and settled it over her shoulders. At the simple pressure of his hands, Meggie's heart popped.

"There." He stepped back. "Warmer?"

"Much," she croaked. The cloak smelled of him, all delicious spice, rugged leather and masculine male.

He was staring at her again, and everywhere his gaze roamed, her body burned.

Helplessly, she found herself imagining his fingers traversing the same ground his eyes had just traveled. Her breasts engorged with heated desire. She was very aware of him as a virile, potent man.

Disconcerted, she stared down at her feet and realized to her chagrin she was wearing only one shoe.

Good grief, why had she just now noticed that? What was the matter with her?

Why didn't he say something?

Why didn't she?

Meggie glanced around the room, desperate to distract herself from the intensity of his scrutiny. The community center was crowded with tourists and townspeople alike, everyone decked out for the lavish, end-of-summer masked costume ball. Excitement and mystery tinged the atmosphere as everyone tried to guess who was who.

The costume theme was "notorious characters from history," and guests wore a wide variety of attire, from Attila the Hun to Bonnie and Clyde.

Animated conversations buzzed around her. A cavalcade of delicious scents wafted from the buffet—onions, garlic, rosemary, freshly baked bread, a banquet for the senses. Liam Kilstrom, the disc jockey from KCRK—the local radio station her parents owned—spun a kicky, raucous song by Pink that had everyone on their feet. But Meggie couldn't seem to focus on anything except the perplexing pull of the exotic masked stranger and his unwavering stare.

She wished he would cut it out.

Now she could say she knew exactly how a goldfish felt.

Exposed.

He leaned over, picked up her orphaned shoe and indicated her bare foot with a nod. "May I?"

Numbly, Meggie plunked back down in the chair and extended her leg.

Don Juan sank to one knee, cupped her heel in his palm and, like Prince Charming with Cinderella, gently slipped the scarlet shoe onto her foot.

The warmth from his hand was too much. She felt as if she'd slipped into a vat of melted chocolate.

He stood. Unbidden, her gaze tracked a path down the length of him. His body was hard and lean and muscular. A honed body that spoke of time spent outdoors, not lingering behind some desk.

Impressive.

He was a provocative specimen, from his thick unruly black hair, which contrasted starkly with the pristine white of his collar, to his broad-shouldered torso that tapered down to the narrow waistband of those exquisite leather pants.

This was way too much excitement for one night. This evening was supposed to be her coming-out party. The first time she had attended a public function since her divorce six months earlier. The first time she'd done anything remotely social since taking a leave of absence from her job as a pediatric nurse in Seattle.

She'd returned to Bear Creek under the auspices of

helping her mother while she recovered from ankle surgery. But in truth, Meggie had come back to the safety of her hometown in order to regroup and lick her wounds.

She refused to get trapped in a rebound situation. She wasn't about to repeat her past mistakes by falling headlong for some totally inappropriate guy.

You could just have a wild affair.

Impossible.

She felt her face heat at the very suggestion. Meggie Scofield was not a wild affair kinda gal. She was too sensible, too responsible and too darned cautious to leap without looking.

One thing was clear. Because she couldn't seem to trust her own emotions, she had to get away from this guy. Fast.

Grabbing her clutch purse, which had slipped into the crack behind the chair cushion, she jerked a thumb in the direction of the ladies' room.

In a tight whisper she stammered, "I'm gonna...I just gotta...go."

A smile curled his lips, as if her nervousness amused him. He looked as if he might say something else, but Meggie didn't wait to hear it. She darted from the chair and made a beeline for the bathroom, her heart pounding as it never had before.

2

SEVERAL MINUTES LATER her three best friends found her hiding out in the ladies' lounge, head tucked between her knees as she tried not to hyperventilate.

"Meggie! Are you okay?" Kay Freemont Scofield, Meggie's new sister-in-law, settled herself on the sofa next to her and draped an arm around her shoulder.

Woefully, Meggie raised her head. "Fine if you consider a five-alarm hot flash fine."

"Does it have anything to do with that hottie in the Don Juan costume we saw you talking to?" Classy, native New Yorker Kay looked stunning in her Mata Hari costume. Then again Kay, a Charlize Theron look-alike, would be stunning in a tow sack.

"Certainly not. I just got overheated in that crowded room."

"Don Juan looks like he could definitely steam up the sheets. Need an ice pack?" Sassy Sadie Stanhope, dressed as Marie Antoinette, wriggled her eyebrows and parked her fanny in front of the vanity mirror to freshen up her makeup.

"No," Meggie declared, reluctant to admit her helpless attraction. But then she ruined her nonchalant pose by asking, "Do you know who he is?"

"Nope." Kay shook her head. "But he is adorable."

Adorable? That wasn't a label Meggie would have chosen for that studly slab of manhood. Her heel still burned from his touch.

Reaching over, Cammie Jo Lockhart rubbed Don Juan's silk cloak between her fingers. "Cool cape. Did you two play superhero and damsel in distress?"

"Don't be silly, I did not play anything with that man. I was cold. He lent me his cape. End of story."

"Wait a minute. I thought you said you were overheated."

"That was before."

"Before what?" Cammie Jo grinned.

"Before Mr. Hot-Bod draped his cape over her shoulders." Sadie measured off an inch with her thumb and forefinger. "Come on, Megs, are you sure you're not just the teeniest bit interested in him?"

Meggie shook her head. "Okay. So the man is sexy. Big deal. I'll tell you what the real problem is—this costume. I told you guys it was a big mistake. I look like some third-rate hooker. He probably thought I *was* a hooker."

She got up to lean over Sadie's head and peer at her reflection in the vanity mirror. Kay had helped her get ready for the party, and she'd spread enough makeup on Meggie's face to frost a cake.

But at the same time she was protesting, a quiet thrill of pleasure rippled through Meggie. She had managed to attract the attention of a very handsome man. Still, in this racy disguise she felt like an inexperienced driver behind the wheel of a souped-up muscle car.

So much flash. So much power.

So darned much potential for disaster, whispered her voice of reason.

The same confounded voice that had kept her tied to outmoded values for far too many years. The same stick-in-the-mud voice she had desperately tried to quell when she had allowed her friends to talk her into this outrageous costume.

"Don't be silly," Kay said matter-of-factly. "Klondike Kate is the perfect alter ego, and you look fabulous in that bustier."

Meggie twirled, the cape whirling about her waist as she peeked over her shoulder at the mirror. She sighed. "It makes my butt look big."

"Stop cutting yourself down," Kay said. "You've got a great figure."

"Not according to Jesse," she muttered blackly, narrowing her eyes at the reflection of her well-rounded bottom.

"Oh, screw Jesse."

"Not anymore, thank you very much. I'll leave that to the eighteen-year-old groupies," Meggie said in a tart tone that caused Sadie and Cammie Jo to lapse into gales of laughter.

"As well you should." Kay nodded.

Jesse's leaving hadn't hurt nearly as much as his cruel parting shot. He had told her point-blank she was a lousy lay and that's why he had been forced to stray from their marriage bed.

"Face it, Meggie. You're a dud in the sack," he had said, lashing out at her. "Sock puppets are more fun than you."

Meggie winced at the memory. His words hurt because they were true. She wasn't very adventuresome when it came to sex, and she'd always preferred snuggling to the actual act. Not that her ex had been much of a cuddler.

Kay, Sadie and Cammie Jo had rallied around, just as they were now, helping her through the rough spots with too much chocolate and lots of laughter. Most surprisingly, and most comforting of all, however, was the support she'd gotten from Jesse's stepbrother, Caleb.

Caleb was such a sweet guy, concerned that she might be humiliated or worried that the rest of the family thought ill of her. He had come to see her at her parents' house right after he'd found out about the divorce, just to assure her that everyone understood and sympathized with her.

"You've got to stop judging yourself on what other people think," Sadie advised, "and find your authentic self."

"Thank you, Dr. Phil."

"Sadie's right. You are much too good for Jesse's sorry ass." Kay picked up on Meggie's sadness.

In a moment of weakness, she had confessed to Kay the whole sordid details of their breakup, which included finding black thong panties that definitely weren't hers dangling from the kitchen ceiling fan.

"You shouldn't let him squash your self-esteem. If I can come out of my shell, so can you," Cammie Jo said. After meeting her husband-to-be, bush pilot Mack McCaulley, she had recently been through a startling transformation of her own.

"Cammie Jo makes an excellent point." Sadie nodded. "You need to reclaim your womanhood. Declare your independence. Redefine your sexuality. It's way past time you started to live a little.''

Live a little.

Just the mention of those three short words caused Meggie's heart to flutter with anticipation. She thought of Don Juan and her stomach did cartwheels. Did she have the guts to go back out there and start a conversation with him?

A conversation that might lead to...where?

An edginess nibbled at Meggie, challenging her to do something forbidden. She felt concurrently hot and cold and bizarrely excited.

''If you've got it, flaunt it,'' Kay said.

''I'm not much of a flaunter.''

''It's time you started. You've spent too much of your life taking care of other people. Your mother's ankle has healed. You're going back home to Seattle tomorrow to begin your new life as a single woman. What better time to start taking care of numero uno than right this minute?''

Kay spoke words of wisdom, but Meggie felt uncomfortable admitting her vulnerability. She was a nurse. She was supposed to be the strong, reliable one. She blew off her shortcomings with a laugh, pretending a sharp sticker of emotional pain did not skitter low in her belly.

It wasn't so much sadness over Jesse's betrayal. Truth be told, she was relieved to be out of the unhappy union. Their marriage had died long before the divorce; she just hadn't had the gumption to bring it to its natural conclusion.

Rather, the tight coil of anxiety resulted from realizing she'd wasted so much time trying to be what

Jesse had wanted her to be in order to hang on to something that wasn't right in the first place.

A nurturer by nature, she'd never put her own needs first. Meggie had spent her entire life looking after others in one way or another. As a kid, she had taken in every stray animal she had stumbled across, and she'd helped her mother care for her invalid grandmother. As an adult, her natural ease in providing moral, emotional and physical support had led to a career in nursing, which was a source of constant pride.

Unfortunately, her need to be needed had also led her into an unsatisfactory marriage. She'd fallen for Jesse because he was everything she was not. Lively, animated, adventuresome, freewheeling. He played in a hip-hop band, drove fast cars and was always surrounded by people.

She had mistakenly believed he could give her the courage she lacked, while at the same time convincing herself she could offer him stability and security. She'd been drawn to the fact that he'd needed her, but not long after their wedding, the problems surfaced.

All too clearly now, she could see her mistakes.

What she'd once perceived as Jesse's ability to take life nice and easy was in actuality irresponsibility. He was always on the road, leaving her at home to take care of everything—the bills, the house, the cars. She'd been as good as single for the past five years, but without the freedom to choose for herself what kind of life she really wanted.

"Remember," Kay said, uncannily reading her mind. "The best revenge is a life well lived. Come on, Meggie. Let your hair down. Don't be ashamed to explore."

"You're absolutely right." Sounded good, anyway.

"This is your chance. You've been stagnating and you need something to snap you out of the doldrums. Don't be nervous about spreading your wings. Now is the time to fly." Sadie threw in her two cents worth.

Why not? Under the protection of her Klondike Kate guise, Meggie could flirt with Don Juan to her heart's content. No one in Bear Creek, other than her three friends, would ever know whose face lurked behind the red-feathered mask. She was anonymous.

Why that thought should thrill her so, she had no idea, but it did.

She would flirt with Don Juan and dance with him.

And?

Who knew? She might do something totally out of character for her, like make out with the guy in a darkened alcove.

Live a little.

Take a chance.

Carpe diem.

Just the idea of taking a walk on the wild side caused her throat to constrict and her palms to perspire.

"Go back out there and flirt with Don Juan," Kay insisted. "You've got nothing to lose."

"Yeah," Sadie agreed. "What's the worst that can happen? He has no idea who you really are. Play the game. Have fun. You deserve it."

"And just in case..." Kay opened her Gucci handbag and produced a roll of condoms.

"Kay!" Scandalized, Meggie slapped a hand over her mouth. She had never in her life had a one-night stand. Did she dare start now?

"Always be prepared." Kay grinned and slipped the condoms into Meggie's purse.

"I don't need those. I'm not going to be doing anything like that."

"You never know what might pop up." Kay winked. "Better safe than sorry."

Meggie nibbled her bottom lip. She was very open to suggestion right now—susceptible, vulnerable, fragile—and she knew it.

But that knowledge couldn't quell her long-ignored need to shake up her complacent world. She would take Jesse's betrayal and use it as a stepping-stone to a whole new Meggie. Why not?

And here were her dear friends, supporting her, encouraging her, egging her on with their spunky you-go-girl attitude. They recognized that she needed a little masculine admiration to repair her tattered ego. It seemed they knew her better than she knew herself.

She wanted this, Meggie realized with a start. She was twenty-nine years old, newly divorced and fighting off a deep-seated dread that life was sprinting by her at a dead run. This might be her last chance to really explore her limits and relish her youth.

Question was, did she have the courage to go for the gusto? Was she brave enough to reach for what she wanted? To explore the secret sexual fantasies she'd never shared with anyone? A weird sense of panic scampered through her. Did she possess enough chutzpah to initiate something wickedly wonderful with Don Juan?

Or was she going to end up a lonely old spinster with a houseful of Siamese cats, pining sadly for what might have been?

Take a risk. Who knows what you'll discover about yourself? whispered an audacious voice in the back of her mind—the voice she'd spent a lifetime denying because it scared her so.

Go for it. You may never have a chance like this again.

"*METROPOLITAN* WOULD LIKE to thank the Bachelors of Bear Creek for taking out that wonderful advertisement. You guys single-handedly boosted the magazine's circulation by twenty percent." Kay Scofield stood on the stage at the back of the community center, microphone in hand, her husband, Quinn, by her side.

She smiled at Quinn with a shining love that made Caleb's gut hitch with jealousy. All the bachelors had found someone to love except him.

"And on a more personal note..." Kay stared deeply into her husband's eyes "...I want to thank you for making me the happiest woman in the world, Quinn. I'm honored to be your wife."

"Aww!" The crowd sighed in unison when Kay stood on tiptoes to kiss her husband, who was dressed, appropriately enough for his size, as Paul Bunyon.

"This party is also to celebrate the impending marriage of Sadie Stanhope and Jake Gerard." Kay scanned the audience. "Sadie and Jake, please take a bow."

Liam, the disc jockey, shone the spotlight on Jake

and Sadie, who were swaying together in the middle of the dance floor. Jake waved his hand and Sadie blew kisses to the crowd.

Caleb shook his head and grinned to himself. Those two were a pair. He'd never thought fun-loving Jake would settle down, but Jake had met his match in Sadie.

"Wedding is December 16 at our B and B," Jake said. "Remember, you're all invited."

"And Cammie Jo Lockhart and Mack McCaulley," Kay continued, "are you out there?" She raised a hand to her forehead to scan the crowd.

Liam flashed the spotlight to the corner of the room, interrupting the two lovebirds in the throes of a deep kiss.

Someone whooped with delight. Cammie Jo blushed and ducked her head. Mack grinned like a kid caught with his hand in the cookie jar. The audience applauded.

In a very short time Bear Creek had changed considerably, and mostly for the better. Not only had Caleb's three best friends gotten hitched or engaged, but the population had grown from fifteen hundred to almost two thousand.

Some of the ladies that had arrived in response to the ad had fallen in love with Alaska and decided to stay, even though they hadn't found a husband. Some of the fellows from surrounding communities had moved in, hoping to catch the eye of one of those ladies. Bear Creek was growing and changing from a summer tourist resort into a real town. Part of Caleb liked the changes. Another part of him feared his hometown might one day lose its rustic appeal as an increase in population tamed the wilderness.

''The ad's success rate stands at seventy-five percent,'' Kay continued, once everyone had settled down. ''That's pretty darned impressive, but the magazine would love a hundred percent success rate. There's only one bachelor left. Caleb, where are you?''

He took a step back, not interested in being thrust into the spotlight.

''Caleb?'' Kay called out. ''Come on up here.''

That's when he realized no one knew he was dressed as Don Juan. Relief washed through him. All he had to do was keep quiet. He didn't want Klondike Kate to know he was the millionaire bachelor, which would seriously alter her perception of him. At least for tonight he wished to remain incognito.

''Caleb, where are you?'' Kay coaxed.

Meggie cocked her head to one side and peered through the crowd, hoping to spy her ex-stepbrother-in-law. She hadn't seen much of Caleb this summer—he'd been too busy fending off love-starved ladies, while she'd been sequestered at home taking care of her mother.

But since she was catching the first plane out of Anchorage tomorrow morning, this would be the last chance she'd have to say goodbye. She was very happy that her divorce from Jesse hadn't caused any hard feelings between them; Caleb was a good, stable, honest man. The kind of guy she should have married.

''Caleb?'' Kay repeated for the third time, but he did not appear. ''Anyone seen Caleb?''

Meggie wasn't surprised, although she felt disappointed. Caleb wasn't much of one for parties or crowds.

"Well, I guess all you single ladies are out of luck. Seems our most eligible bachelor has flown the coop," Kay said. "But on a positive note, the buffet is now open for business. Enjoy, everyone."

Meggie kept searching the crowd, but when her gaze landed on Don Juan, she forgot all about Caleb.

Don Juan was talking to a razor-thin woman in a black cat suit. Meggie immediately felt fat and dumpy in contrast. She shook off that feeling. She wasn't going to think negatively. So what if she was a size twelve and not a size two? Just because her ex had preferred rail-thin women, that didn't mean everyone did.

Don Juan turned slightly, and she could see his stunning profile made all the more intriguing by the camouflage of his mask. She stared at his full, ripe mouth.

What would he taste like?

She knew the answer deep within the most hidden parts of her. He would taste like sin. She pursed her lips and slowly released a pent-up sigh.

He angled his head, caught sight of her from his peripheral vision and smiled very, very slightly, as if he harbored a hundred sexy secrets. No one else in the building would have noticed the glance, the smile, so subtle was his execution.

But Meggie did.

Go on over and put on a show. Pretend to be Klondike Kate.

She wanted to, but she was afraid of so many things. Like making a mistake, or getting in too deep.

How deep could you sink, Meggie? You're leaving town tomorrow morning, never to see Don Juan again.

Not knowing exactly how to deal with her unexpected sexual desires, she sought sublimation. The buffet beckoned. She hurried over to the table, picked up a plate and started down the serving line.

With a cocktail fork, she leaned over to spear a moist, pink shrimp, but before she could retrieve her succulent prize, someone on the other side of the table got to it first.

"Hey," she protested, then raised her head and caught Don Juan's stare head-on.

He stood before her, the fat, slick shrimp impaled on his fork. Leaning forward, he dangled the seafood mere inches from her lips. Damn if he didn't possess a small, wicked smile tilting up one corner of his mouth.

Meggie's stomach did the hula and her knees loosened. She had the sudden urge to sit right down on the floor so she wouldn't topple over from his body heat.

"I will share with you, belladonna," he murmured with his captivating Spanish accent, rolling the word *belladonna* around in his mouth, savoring it as if it was the finest Belgian chocolate money could buy.

Slowly, Don Juan lowered the shrimp until it lightly brushed her bottom lip. Meggie flicked out her tongue to whisk away a drop of juice. Audibly, he sucked in his breath, his eyes never leaving her face.

Her heart careened into her rib cage, and she felt oddly enchanted. Determined not to let him know exactly how much he had affected her, Meggie shrugged and stepped back.

"On second thought I think I'll skip the shrimp," she said, affecting Klondike Kate's uncultured inflection.

"Why is that?" he whispered. "Are you afraid?"

"Afraid?" She avoided looking into his eyes again. "What's there to be afraid of?"

"Some say shrimp is an aphrodisiac."

"Old wives' tale," she pronounced, really getting into the gold-rush madam's brogue.

"So why not take a bite and see?"

He was flirting with her, no doubt about it. Meggie didn't know what to do. It had been a very long time since someone had flirted so openly with her. She wanted the attention and yet she didn't.

"No, thanks."

"Ahh," he said knowingly. "I understand."

In spite of her best intentions not to meet his eyes again, Meggie had to slip a quick glance his way to see what he was ahhing about. She was immediately sorry she had. Sympathy for her shone on his face.

Damn. She didn't need his pity. She didn't want anyone's pity, and she'd spent the past six months trying to convince everyone in Bear Creek of that fact. Now here was this masked stranger, reading her every emotion as if he truly knew her.

"You've been hurt by love."

She rolled her eyes. "Oh please. Anyone over the age of eighteen has been hurt by love."

"But you've been hurt recently and you're afraid to try again."

"Hush up," she insisted, but her pulse sprinted through her bloodstream.

How could he know this about her? Who was he? Was he from her hometown? If so, then who was he? No local man had ever set her libido to whirling the way this guy did. Bear Creek was too small, everyone too much like family.

"He has made you doubt your desirability as a woman," Don Juan said. "He is a terrible bastard. Do not concern yourself with him."

Her chest suddenly felt tight and she had the strangest urge to laugh and cry all at the same time.

"Look at me," he insisted. "Look me in the eyes and tell me you're not in pain."

For pity's sake. With a sigh of exasperation, Meggie stared him squarely in the face.

And lost herself.

With that warm smile and lusty expression in his eyes, Don Juan made her feel womanly, wanted and appreciated. Cherished. It was a feeling she hadn't experienced in a very, very long time.

Entranced, she felt ensnared in a provocative reverie. A dreamy vagueness settled over her, wrapping her in a warm envelope of altered perception. She didn't know if it was the masks or the wine or Don Juan's solicitous smile, but she experienced a drowsy sense of peace.

Something about him seemed comfortingly familiar, as if she'd met him in another life. Except Meggie didn't believe in that stuff. Even though she couldn't exactly explain why, she felt safe in his presence.

Don Juan was the tonic she needed. The physical vehicle for her emotional healing. This magnetic man could be the cure for the psychic malaise that had dogged her for years.

In that instant, Meggie knew she was going to sleep with him.

MAGIC.

His costume was magic. It had to be. Caleb could think of no other explanation for his miraculous ease with the beautiful mystery woman. Wearing the mask and fake mustache was a liberating experience. He could be anyone. He could say and do anything.

Hell's bells, he felt as if he were channeling Don Juan himself.

He was breathing hard, and roughly, the shrimp still dangling from his outstretched fork as he waited for Klondike Kate's sweet, crimson lips to part and sheathe the tender morsel.

Their gazes locked. Who was she really?

She was breathing as hard as he, the gentle swell of her chest rising and falling in a mesmerizing rhythm. Holding him enthralled.

She reminded him vaguely of someone. But who? His mind probed the question but arrived at no answer.

Kate's green eyes were lively and intelligent, the top half of her face hidden by the red-feathered mask. She wielded her tongue like an instrument of torture, touching it lightly against her upper lip as if purposely trying to make him lose control.

The visual impact slugged him. Hard.

His blood flowed hot and viscous through his veins. The way she gazed at him, like a curious innocent intent on exploring a brave new world, clutched something deep inside him and refused to turn it loose.

In that brief endless moment, as they faced off across the buffet table, the wet, pink shrimp as the prize, Caleb memorized everything about her not swaddled by the mask. The way she smelled of fresh summer rain, making him ache to bury his face in the curve of her neck. The fine brown freckles that lightly decorated her upper chest, exposed so engagingly by that red bustier. The irregular pounding of her pulse at her jawline. The sweet ruby bow of her lips.

And the completely gut-scorching realization that beneath the satin and lace of her flimsy undergarment, her nipples were standing at erect attention.

He almost groaned aloud.

''Excuse me,'' Genghis Kahn interrupted, leaning across the table between them, tortilla chip in hand. ''Could I get at that crab dip?''

Flustered, Caleb moved aside at the same time Klondike Kate blushed prettily, smiled and turned away.

Damn. The moment was lost.

Or was it?

Caleb ate the shrimp himself, hurried around to her side of the buffet table and boldly took her elbow. Instantly, his fingers tingled at the warmth of her soft skin. He pressed his mouth next to her delicate ear and murmured in a muffled growl, ''What is your name?''

She lowered lashes so dark and long they brushed against her mask with a whispery rasp. ''Now, now, that's not part of the game.''

''And what is the game?'' he asked, his voice thick with feeling.

''Secrecy. Anonymity. Mystery. That's the fun.''

''You're not going to tell me your name?''

''My name is Klondike Kate. Don Juan, I presume?''

He took the hand she offered him and pressed the back of it to his lips, as if he'd performed the courtly gesture a million times. He clicked his heels and bowed.

''At your service.''

''I am flattered. The famous lothario gracing the halls of my brothel. Perhaps, Señor Juan, we can teach each other a few tricks.''

Ah, but she was extraordinary. One minute blushing shyly, the next sassily playing at being a brothel madam in that whispery tone that obviously wasn't her real voice. Just like him, she was playing a part. Her words hung between them like a physical entity, their meaning sinking into his brain one vivid movie-reel image at a time.

She wanted to teach him a few tricks.

Holy macaroni!

He was going to combust right there on the spot. What a game. Suddenly, he knew he had to get her alone.

''Wrap up your plate,'' he said, barely remembering to keep up his Spanish accent. ''Take it to go. We'll have a picnic in the forest.''

''The forest?'' Her eyes widened and for a moment he thought he'd panicked her and she was going to back out of their little masquerade.

"Twenty yards right outside this door, and you're in the Tongass National Forest."

"You don't say."

He waited. "Well?"

"I don't think I'm really in the mood for food," she murmured.

"No?"

"My appetite is of a different nature."

Caleb thought he was going to break out in a sweat right then and there. "Mine as well."

"You go on ahead." She cast a surreptitious glance around the room and settled her plate on an empty table. "And I will follow. One can never be too careful. There might be spies."

"Spies?" He knew this was just part of her charade, but damn if he wasn't turned on by the thought of being observed. "Who is watching us?"

"Why, any number of your women, or my men." She winked. "We must keep our clandestine affair secret. No sense making our other lovers jealous."

Caleb gulped.

Potential scenarios tumbled through his head, each more stimulating than the next. He was cast iron hard, and the leather pants did nothing to arrest his arousal. All she had to do was glance down and she would know his every illicit thought.

"Go," she urged in an imperative whisper that charged his libido. "Hurry, before we are spotted. I will meet you in the forest. Wait for me."

She pressed her hand to his forearm, setting off monster ripples of sensation straight up his shoulder and into his chest, to his belly and beyond—a taut-ness, an electrical impulse, a dynamic combustion that made it difficult to string two words together.

"Don't stand me up," he growled.

"I won't. Now just go." She pushed him toward the front door.

Then, before he could respond, she turned and disappeared out the side exit adjacent to the stage.

Caleb had never done anything like this before—scheduled an amorous rendezvous with a woman he did not know and might never meet again. He was by nature a quiet, solitary man guided more by his brains than his body or his heart. But ever since putting on that Don Juan costume, he'd been transformed.

Tonight he was different.

And so was she.

Caleb sensed this was as much an erotic adventure for the mysterious Klondike Kate as it was for him, and he was bound and determined to make it a night neither of them would ever forget.

3

WHAT IN THE HELL had she just done?

Had she gone completely mental? Could the stress of the past six months have caused her to take leave of her senses and chase after the first man who showed her some attention? So what if Don Juan was sexy and handsome as Hades, and apparently more than willing to indulge in flirtatious games? None of this explained her uncharacteristic behavior.

Her brain squawked, telling her how foolish she was to take such a chance, but a tiny voice in the back of her head whispered, "Seize the moment. For once in your life, Megan Marie Scofield, live a little."

Then again, maybe her real motivation was more of a compulsion than any sincere desire to take charge of her life. From the moment she'd spied him lounging so lawlessly against the wall, she'd felt...well, something special.

As she picked her way through the forest in the twilight, her condom-filled clutch purse tucked beneath her arm, Don Juan's cape flapping about her shoulders, her heart rate thudded faster and faster, headed straight for the danger zone. Still, she couldn't seem to make herself turn around and go back to the party.

She was like a songbird unaware it had been caged

until one day the door was left open and the opportunity to fly presented itself. Should she take wing and explore the brave new world extending before her? Or stay safely hunched on her perch, watching life pass her by?

The answer wasn't difficult, even to her conflicted brain. Don Juan was simply too exciting, and too good-looking, the prospect of making love with him far too sweet to be denied.

Besides, when was the last time she had been so sexually aroused? Never? Ever? Could he actually teach her to let go of her hang-ups in bed? She owed it to herself to find out.

Her shoes bogged in the mossy carpet of undergrowth beneath the towering hemlocks and swaying Sitka spruces. She was glad she'd taken the time to change into the sensible footwear she kept stashed in the trunk of her car.

A blueberry bush, devoid now of its berry harvest, grazed her leg, startling her. The air was heavy with moisture and she heard nothing beyond the gurgling creek and the faint hmm of voices and music from the party she'd left behind.

Oh dear. Where was Don Juan? She had expected him to stay close to the perimeters of the forest, where she could find him easily.

"Come."

She heard the whisper, low and seductive. She wasn't certain from which direction it originated.

He was concealing himself from her, ratcheting the game up a notch.

Meggie bit down on her bottom lip, tasted the opulent flavor of her own lust. She was nervous, confused, curious and extremely turned on.

What was going to happen next?

"Don Juan?" She heard a faint rustling in the trees, then nothing more.

In the phantom of rapidly dwindling daylight, she walked through the forest, pushing back vegetation, stepping gingerly over tree roots, eager not to fall and sprain her ankle. A sprained ankle would definitely blow the moment.

And the last thing she wanted was a dose of reality. She wanted to escape, as she had of late in the pages of fantasy romance novels. What she longed for was to disappear in this dreamy netherworld. She could easily envisage unicorns and fairies, woodland sprites playing flutes and dancing around magic toadstools. She ached for a pretend world of virginal maidens, stalwart knights and deep, undying passion.

Her friends had regaled her with their own tales of acute throbbing desire. Of lust at first sight. Of being drawn helplessly into earthly pleasures beyond emotional control. She'd never really believed those stories, even though she had desperately wanted to. Hadn't known such intensity of physical feeling was possible.

Until now.

She stopped walking.

He'd been here. On this path. Right where she was standing. She could smell him. As individual as a fingerprint, his scent hung in her nostrils like a primal memory.

A faint fear, tinged with escalating anticipation, pinched her solar plexus in a dazzling heat that hastened her footsteps and sent her heart staggering headlong into a restless, thrashing rhythm.

Another step deeper into the gloaming. Another and then another.

Twigs crunched beneath her feet. A fingered fern crept across her ankle. A bubble of fear caused her to jump, and then laugh at her own spooked state.

Nothing to be afraid of. She was in control of the situation. She wasn't little Red Riding Hood evading the Big, Bad Wolf. She could turn if she wished and go back to the party. Nothing was keeping her here except her own inquisitiveness and her escalating imagination.

Walking up a slight embankment, she glanced left and then right, saw only the tall, thin thrust of tree trunks and the full orange moon rising over the horizon.

Was it possible to breathe any faster and not faint from hyperventilation? Could her stomach possibly squeeze any tighter? Could her knees grow any weaker and not dissolve into noodle soup?

He was enticing her, this man. And she wanted him to capture her, no matter how sinfully foolish her subterranean desires.

Goose bumps pricked a warning, raising the hairs on her forearms and the nape of her neck.

He was near. She could feel him.

CALEB WAS IN HIS ELEMENT. The forest. The wilderness. Home.

He inhaled her on the cool evening breeze. Sweet, ripe, glowing. Soap, perfume, saltiness. The luscious aroma stirred a pulsating pressure of impulsive hunger deep within his masculinity.

Like predator to prey her scent drew him. His mouth watered and every fiber of his being grew taut, every male sense alerted to the wondrous female encroaching on his territory.

Relentlessly, her womanly bouquet lured him. Silently her body entreated, *Come to me.* Pheromones. Natures mating call. As surely as any hapless male moth enticed to a flame, she ensnared him with her spinning scent song.

He could not resist.

Through the copse of trees he caught a flash of crimson, a glimmer of her auburn hair, the sound of her teasing laugh.

"I see you," he crooned in his heavy Spanish accent.

"Come and get me," she dared, and darted from his sight.

He heard the sounds of her feet crashing through the woods. Grinning, he followed.

The hunt was on.

Every cell in his body strummed to life in a way he'd never experienced. Feverish heat punched through his system like a fist through a paper bag, tattering any shred of civilized behavior. A savage hunger dogged him, his feral passions mounting in shocking disregard for decorum.

He wanted her—in a way he'd never wanted another. Not even Meggie in his teenage years.

He moved with long, easy loping strides, knowing he could effortlessly outlast her.

This was his every naughty fantasy come true.

SHE'D CAUGHT A GLIMPSE of him back there. Silhouetted at the top of the embankment, with the fat full moon at his back, he'd been watching her with hooded eyes.

Consumed by both thrill and trepidation, she slipped away the minute she realized he had spotted her, too. She had issued a challenge that reverberated in the silent air.

Come and get me.

She pushed through the undergrowth and then realized with a start that she was lost. It had been a long time since she'd visited the Tongass, and she had no idea which direction Bear Creek lay.

Licking her lips, she furtively scanned the forest, every muscle in her body tense with anticipation. In the moonlight, she spotted a clearing just ahead of her.

She moved toward the opening, not knowing if she should go there, risk exposing herself to him and foiling the fun, or stay secluded and draw out their play. But she needed to get her bearings and discover her location.

Cautiously, she emerged and peeped through the trees to see a pond shimmering in the moon glow. Beside the pond squatted a small skaters' cabin, meticulously maintained by the forest rangers. As kids she and Quinn, Caleb, Jake and Mack had shared many happy memories there. Ice skating on the frozen pond, laughing, joking, teasing each other, and then slipping inside the cabin to warm up with hot chocolate and marshmallows toasted over a fire in the black potbellied stove.

Her heart gave a strange tug of nostalgia at the memory. As a young woman, she couldn't wait to leave Bear Creek for big-city lights. She'd thought she would never miss anything about living in the isolated wilds of Alaska. But seeing that little cabin again reminded her that Bear Creek could provide her with something special that Seattle never could—cherished childhood memories.

She heard the rustle of leaves and slipped back into the sheltering trees.

Don Juan was behind her. Coming quickly but quietly, as if he knew every step of the path.

Hide! a giddy, childish impulse urged her.

Trying her best not to giggle and give away the game too soon, Meggie looked for a good hiding place. Trees trunks loomed on either side of her, tall and imposing but narrow and thin.

She crawled behind a spruce, hoping that if she stood sideways and stayed as still as possible he wouldn't immediately spot her in the gloom. Pulling herself tall, she pressed flat against the trunk, closed her eyes tight, strained to hear, and waited.

Nothing. Except for the wind whispering faintly through the trees and her own blood roaring in her ears, there was only silence.

She held her breath.

Her heart lub-dubbed

Had he gone? Given up already?

Oh, no. Please don't let that be so.

She wanted to look, to move, to breathe, but hated to end the suspense. Not just yet.

Sweat popped out on her brow despite the chill.

An uneasy minute passed.

Still nothing.

Finally, unable to hold her breath any longer, she let out a soft whoosh of air and inhaled deeply.

She waited, breathing hard.

That's when his viselike arms clamped around her waist.

Meggie let out a shriek, the sound reverberating throughout the forest, and dropped her clutch purse. But he did not let her go. In fact, those ropy, muscled arms wrapped more tightly around her.

"You are mine now, slippery minx." His lyrical Spanish accent stroked her ears, transporting her deeper into the magical dream.

He was standing behind her, securely holding her bottom pressed flush against his groin. She could feel the heat and hardness of his throbbing erection through the inconsequential restriction of his leather pants. His hand came perilously close to her womanhood, cloaked so thinly by the satiny tap pants. Her flesh felt seared, achy, desperate.

She wanted to see his face. To read the expression of the eyes beneath that mask. As if intercepting her thoughts, he spun her around, clasping her wrists in his hands, and held her restrained.

"You make my blood race," he said.

God, she loved the way he'd been masterfully setting the tone from the moment he'd approached her at the buffet table. He seemed to know exactly what she needed to hear.

Two could play this game. Meggie swallowed hard, valiantly tilted her chin and met his gaze. "*You* make my body ache."

"And you bring me to my knees."

She saw sexual hunger in his eyes, yes, but tenderness as well. He caressed her with his gaze, as if he knew precisely where to touch and how to torment her with sweet, exquisite pleasure.

"You're feeding into my most taboo fantasies," she told him.

"I know."

"I want to feed yours as well. What are your most wicked desires, Don Juan?" Meggie thrilled to her own bravery. "How can I captivate you?"

He pulled her flush against his strong, solid chest and she inhaled the arousing scent of a man in his prime. They generated so much body heat, pressed together, that Meggie could almost feel the steam rising from their contact.

"Can't you guess? I like to play games."

Anonymity had all sorts of benefits, she decided, nuzzling his neck. She was catching the early morning flight to Seattle. The whole population of Bear Creek was inside the community center. No one would ever know she had slipped into the forest with Don Juan. It was just their little secret.

"But we must make sure neither of us does anything to truly scare the other," he said. "Agreed? Nothing too freaky."

"So you're kinky, but not freaky."

"Exactly."

"No S and M."

"No."

"Bondage?"

"Not unless you want it."

Meggie licked her lips. "Maybe just a little."

He chuckled. "We need a word. Or a sign. In case things go too far."

"You're right."

"How about something simple, like 'enough'?"

"All right. Things get out of hand and if either one of us cries 'enough,' the other backs off."

"Agreed."

"Okay, the ground rules are set. What next?"

What next indeed?

His lips were so near, his warm wafting across her mouth.

She wanted to ask him what he was going to do next, but the words would not come. If her very life had been threatened she could not have spoken. She could do nothing but wait in suspended animation for the abracadabra magic that would break his spell.

And then he kissed her.

His lips were warm, soft and perfect. Damn, but the man could kiss. She moaned wantonly into his mouth. Not in a thousand years could Meggie have predicted the earth-cracking impact of Don Juan's kiss or her body's out-of-control response to him.

The excitement of pretending to be an accomplished seductress, the scintillating ego boost from Don Juan's admiration, the titillating secrecy of their masks, the sexy hide and seek, the frank discussion of their sexual limits had dissolved into something much more primal than mere play-acting the very moment his lips brushed hers.

The friction of his kiss unraveled every firm lecture she'd given herself about protecting her heart and staying far away from bad boys. Because none of that mattered at this wondrous moment, when the baddest of bad boys was sweetly, tenderly cajoling her with the silky slide of his mouth across hers, taking time and care to draw her deeper, ever deeper into dangerous territory. Meggie had no defenses against his special brand of languid seduction and beguiling charm. And when he carefully eased her back against the trunk of the tall Sitka spruce and slanted her lips more firmly beneath his, she came utterly undone.

No way out. Absolutely none.

For support, she gripped his corded forearms, which were covered only by his thin shirtsleeves, and held on for dear life. Even though their masks rubbed together as they kissed, Meggie had no desire to remove the barricade and reveal herself.

She liked this experience—anonymous, provocative, daring.

This secrecy was what she craved. As Klondike Kate she was a bold, brash, seductive woman who knew lots of sexy tricks. As Meggie, she was an ordinary twenty-nine-year-old nurse who'd been dumped for a younger woman. She wanted to live this fantasy if only for a short while. Wanted to feel feminine and desirable again.

His eager tongue dipped inside to taste her, tormenting her with silken assaults that liquefied her knees and set her nerve endings tingling. Brazenly, she hunted for a more in-depth sampling of him. At the delicious flavor of man and shrimp and red wine, she shivered.

Ah, sweet lover, thy name is Don Juan.

She shouldn't have been so surprised to find he was a man who took his time and did a thorough job. He kissed her with a scrumptious sleepiness, as if he possessed all the time in the universe captured in the flat of his hand. He seemed intent on exploring every indulgence her mouth had to offer, as if he was memorizing every nuance of taste and texture.

And perhaps he was, for Meggie was doing the same, committing every flavor, every smell, every touch to memory. In the days ahead, whenever she felt lonely or dowdy or depressed, she would take out this moment like a treasured photograph and mentally review it over and over and over again.

He pressed his hips closer, making her all too aware of his burgeoning erection, pinning her hard against the tree trunk. The smell of tree and man combined into an earthy, sprucy scent that sent voluptuous flourishes of sensation coursing throughout her eager body.

With his thumb, he traced her jaw, and her skin caught fire. His wide chest was pressed firmly against hers. Beneath the bustier, her breasts swelled and her nipples tightened and ached. His masculine thigh insinuated itself between her trembling legs and she felt his penis, covered by that tight stretch of black leather, grow even harder against the curve of her hip. Heated desire uncoiled deep within her parts most feminine.

She had never kissed a man with a mustache, and the hair on his upper lip was soft and smooth. She'd expected it to be bristly and uncomfortable. Their masks chafed together in a maddening way and she found herself wanting to rip away their disguises, but she was too afraid of what she might find. Too afraid he would no longer want her once the secrecy had been dispelled.

When he took the kiss even deeper, Meggie responded with an enthusiasm that terrified her. Never had she experienced a passion this all-encompassing, spontaneous and fierce. She had never with such careless abandon wanted a man. Not even in her most untamed daydreams.

What was happening to her, the woman who until tonight had never really cared that much about sex? Nothing had ever prepared her for this kind of concentrated, consuming hunger and desperate, painful need. She was flummoxed, stunned by the intensity of what was happening. Without even realizing it, she'd been searching for something to make her feel alive again, and now, here it was. With one explosive kiss Don Juan tapped into her secret yearnings and made her crave more. So very much more.

What had he done?

While her love-famished body wanted to find out where this irresistible delight might lead, her rational brain reminded her that she wasn't the kind of woman who indulged in one-night stands. Neither a madam costume nor a single kiss, no matter how thrilling and mind-bendingly awesome, could change her into someone she wasn't.

Sensing the shift in her mood, Don Juan slowly dragged his lips from hers. He was breathing heavily, his forceful blue eyes locked on her gaze, his mouth glistening wet from her moisture.

"You've stolen my control," he murmured hoarsely into her ear. "And, I fear, my heart as well."

This was part of the game, she reminded herself. He didn't really mean that she'd stolen his heart. Nor did she want him to mean those words. This was about animal attraction, pure and simple. She wasn't prepared for anything else.

To prove her point, she took his hand and lifted his index finger to her lips. In deliberate, measured increments, she slowly took his thick, round digit into the recesses of her mouth.

He groaned. Loudly.

The searing wet velvet of her tongue had him writhing. Oh, she was wickedly good. His cock bulged against his pants and he feared the seam was going to split right open. He couldn't stand this torture a minute longer.

She looked up at him. Caleb watched her irises grow dark as velvet emeralds and her pupils widen with stark, desperate desire. She wanted him. Savagely.

And best of all, she didn't know that he was the wealthy, unattached Bear Creek bachelor. She didn't want him for his money or what he could buy her.

A surge of fire sped through his veins. Her bare thigh brushed his leather-covered one and he heard her hitch in her throat.

Unable to let the moment pass without indulging himself in one of his milder fantasies, he raised his hand and gently glided his rough fingers along the outline of her chin, relishing the soft smoothness of her feminine jaw, wondering what her cheekbones looked like beneath that sexy red-feathered mask.

They were face-to-face and chest-to-chest. A shadowy expression of pent-up passion clouded her gray-green eyes.

He reached up to touch her hair, his fingers almost trembling from the tension that was building layer upon layer, but she blocked his hand with hers.

"No. Don't," she said.

"Why not?"

"It's a wig."

"What color is your real hair?" he asked, aching to dispose of the wig and plunge his fingers through her sleek locks.

"Let's not ruin the fantasy."

"All right."

He cradled her in his arms, all the while plumbing her ripe, rich mouth. She responded in kind, sending the flames of his libido higher and higher with each flick of her fiendish tongue. Her fingers traced enticing circles over his face and along the edge of his mask. He could feel the steady drubbing of her heart. He stared down into her eyes and felt himself falling, falling, falling.

Playfully, Klondike Kate bit his bottom lip and growled low in her throat, sending his control shattering into a million pieces.

"I need...." she whispered, and that was all she said. It was all she needed to say because he understood her perfectly.

"I know."

His arousal matched hers. Their intrepid game had generated a craving in him he feared might never be sated, and he knew without words that she felt the same way.

Her lips parted and her eyes remained transfixed on his as if she were mesmerized. Slowly, she lifted her hands and softly traced her fingertips along his mouth. Her feathered touch triggered a reaction in him so potent he was ready to explode. As the real Don Juan most assuredly would have, Caleb took advantage of the situation and surrendered to his basic male instincts.

He kissed her again.

Soft, slow and sweet. Gently, tenderly. He knew if he didn't approach this with care, his control would be shot.

Easy. Take it easy.

But what an almost impossible task it was not to slake their desire with rough, spontaneous pleasure.

"The skaters' cabin," she whispered.

"What?"

She nodded toward the clearing. "I saw a skaters' cabin near the pond. This time of year it's sure to be empty, and far more comfortable than the forest floor."

He stared at her, incredulous. "Are you saying what I think you're saying?"

Bending down, she retrieved her fallen purse, tucked it under her arm, then raised her head to meet his gaze.

"Take me," she said.

4

HE SCOOPED HER into his arms, carried her through the forest and into the clearing.

It felt like a dream, a fantasy, a fairy-tale romance.

Without the happily ever after ending, of course. But that was okay. She didn't believe in happily ever after anymore. What she believed in now was living in the moment.

She wanted wild, mind-blowing sex and lots of it. She wanted to prove once and for all that she was not a lousy lay. She wanted to explore, experiment and enjoy. She wanted to reach for and achieve her maximum potential as a woman.

His boots clattered on the wooden steps to the cabin. Giggling, she reached out to open the door and he carried her over the threshold like a virgin bride—cherished, treasured, prized.

The cabin, which would have no electricity until the pond froze over for the winter and Caleb or one of the other naturalists brought over a generator from the ranger's station, was awash in darkness.

Don Juan set her on her feet and put out a hand to steady her. Even with moonlight slanting across the wooden floor, she could barely make out the shape of a sofa pushed against the wall. Then he closed the door behind them, smothering all light and plunging them into blackness so thick Meggie caught her breath. The utter darkness disoriented her. It was too dense, too absolute.

His heady masculine scent enveloped her, drowning out the musty, stale cabin smell. Leather, oranges, cinnamon, licorice and a bracing woodsy aroma. His large hand tightened around hers and he slowly waltzed her toward the sofa. They knew they'd arrived at their destination when their shins brushed against the vinyl material. He eased her down on the seat, then let go of her hand and stepped away.

"Don Juan?" Fear and excitement in an invigorating combination charged through her.

Nothing.

She inhaled shakily. The vinyl was cool and slick against her barely clothed bottom. Meggie strained to hear sounds of him moving. A whispered breath, a creaky floorboard.

"Are you still there?"

Nothing.

Then from out of the ether, a heavy hand settled on her right knee.

She jerked.

Because she could neither see nor hear anything, the hand seemed disconnected, detached, the touch of a phantom lover straight from some erotic hallucination. Warm fingers crept up her knee to her inner thigh.

She tensed, with anticipation or apprehension; she couldn't really say which. The feelings surging through her were electrified, distorted by the sensation of both time and place suspended. Nothing felt real, and yet at the same moment her body hummed with heightened intensity that channeled all her focus to this minute stroking of her skin.

The hand continued, moving upward to skim over her bustier to her waist, and finally stopping to lightly caress her tormented breasts through the stiff lacy material.

No more!

She couldn't tolerate idly waiting. She had to participate in this exquisite teasing. Palms extended, she reached out for him and found his chest. She hissed in air when her fingertips grazed bare, muscled skin and she realized he'd discarded his shirt. Her fingers sank into the soft tuft of chest hair, and the strangeness of his body heightened the dark fantasies revolving through her head.

The texture of his skin, the sculpted configuration of his musculature felt alien but oddly right. She and her unfamiliar lover were alone—in the dark, deep forest, in a deserted cabin. Her normally taciturn body had become wickedly willful, silently begging for more mystery, more suspense. She knew neither this man nor her new self that his caresses had unearthed. And she liked the indefiniteness of it all.

Her hands roamed, learning this different man by the sense of touch. His flesh was damp and hot beneath her palms. The heaviness of his breathing filled her ears, and as she kneaded first his chest and then his shoulders, she felt his fingers work the numerous tiny hooks at the back of her bustier.

Meggie explored him thoroughly, touching here, there, everywhere.

She sensed the raw energy pulsing through his pores. He untied the cape from around her neck. She felt the bustier fall apart in the back, experienced the blaze of his hot, wet mouth as he planted it on her sensitive shoulder blade.

"Are you sure this is what you want?" he asked. "To lie with me?"

He was giving her a way out. She was eternally grateful for his consideration, his kindness in fact heightening her desire for him.

"I'm sure."

"I would hate for you to have regrets."

"No regrets. I promise."

"What would you like?" he whispered. "I want to please you."

"Being with you and playing this game pleases me."

"I need more information. I need specifics."

"Like what? I'm not sure what you mean."

"Where should I touch you? And how? Soft? Hard? Slow? Quick?"

"Anything." She moaned softly and arched into the curve of his body. She wished to sample it all. "Everything."

"You are an adventuresome woman."

"Thanks to you, I am now."

She shivered at the wonder of what was happening. An electric power gushed between them, a vital power strong enough to light the whole of Alaska. They needed neither lamp nor torch. Their passion gave them the vision to see each other as they really were.

Open, vulnerable, ready.

"Where shall we begin?" he whispered.

"Kisses. Lots of kisses."

"Hmm." He pulled her onto his lap so that she was facing forward, her bare back flush against his naked chest, her legs astride his leather-clad thighs. "A very good start."

And then, for what seemed like an eternity of bliss, he kissed her. Brief, velvety kisses on the back of her neck, over her shoulders, down her spine. She tossed her restless head back and he kissed her jaw, her ear, her throat.

He shifted her position, turning her around until they faced each other in the darkness. The sizable bulge in his pants grew harder against her silk-covered womanhood as he planted long, moist kisses on her lips, her chin and the hot pulse throbbing at her collarbone.

Lower and lower he roved, moving her for comfort as he went. First kissing, then licking and at last gently nipping a trail from her neck to her nipples and down her rib cage to her smooth, flat belly. She ended up with her back on the vinyl couch cushion and his taut male body positioned over her, one leg planted on either side of her thighs.

Meggie groaned. "No fair," she whispered. "My turn to tease you. What do you like?"

"Talk dirty to me," he whispered. "Tell me exactly what you'd like for me to do to you."

"Oh, my." Meggie felt the color drain from her face. She wasn't sure she could be *that* boldly uninhibited.

Dull in bed.

The mean-spirited words rang in her head.

Do it. Tell him what you want.

Meggie panted, short and hard, at the thought.

"Tell me," he insisted in a commanding tone that curled her toes.

"I...I can't."

"Why not?"

"I don't know how."

"Open your mouth and say the words."

She hesitated.

"What are you afraid of?"

"That I won't do it right," she confessed.

"Why would you think that?"

She shrugged.

"Let me guess. Some jerk you've been with has misled you about your desirability."

"He said I was dull in bed."

"Dull! You?" Don Juan's vehement reaction warmed her heart. "You are anything but dull. Now talk to me."

"I don't have the guts."

"Yes, you do. Let me hear you say it."

Pretend you're Klondike Kate. She's not dull. Forget the past. Lose yourself. This isn't really real. It's just a dream. Play-acting.

"What do you want?" His low, husky Spanish accent dragged her into the fantasy. She could do this. She would prove that she was brave and exciting and wildly sexual.

Meggie swallowed. "Take off my panties."

"That's good. Very good."

In an instant he slid the silk of her tap pants down her hips, past her knees to her ankles and then over her shoes. A blast of air cooled her heated flesh and she shivered.

"Now what?" he asked.

"Finger me."

"Where?"

"Down there."

"Down where?" She heard the teasing tone of amusement in his voice.

"You know."

"Down here?" He lightly entangled his fingers in the curly hairs at the juncture between her legs.

"Lower." She was panting so hard she could scarcely speak.

His three middle fingers slid over the slick mound of her womanhood and edged toward her aching center. One finger went left, one right, the other straight down the middle.

"Here?"

She nodded, breathless.

"Shall I go on?"

"Uh-huh," she whimpered.

"Say it."

"I...I..."

His face was pressed against her ear, his leather mask rubbing her cheek. She could see absolutely nothing; the darkness was as pure as her desire. Gulping, she squeezed her eyes tightly closed. The hypersensitive sensations spurring through her groin were incredible.

"You've got to tell me or it won't happen."

Say it, Meggie!

Oh, the risks she was taking, the things she was learning about herself.

Dull no more.

"I want to feel your fingers inside me," she said, surprising herself with a strong voice of authority.

He obeyed, sinking his middle digit deep within her warm recess. Meggie gasped out loud and clutched his hair in both her fists.

"You're so wet," he whispered. "So hot."

She tightened her muscles around his finger and his responding groan made her smile into the darkness.

He raised up to kiss her again, his body wedged between her and the back of the sofa, his mouth searching for hers as his inquisitive finger continued gently to investigate her delicate nook. When she arched her pelvis against his hand, he chuckled with satisfaction.

Stroking, rubbing, massaging.

The pressure built inside her like a balloon being blown up...and up...and up...to the point where one more expanse of air would cause it to explode.

Then he stopped and removed his hand.

Meggie cried out in despair. "Don't torture me."

"Do you want me to make you come?" he asked.

She pushed her hips higher and whimpered, low and impulsive.

"Tell me."

"I want you to make me come. Please, please, please. Make me come now."

Caleb's ego soared. He tenderly sucked on her bottom lip while slowly moving his finger in and out, in and out of her magnificent softness. Her moans spiraled steadily, filling the empty blackness with her throaty, feminine noise until his ears rang with the splendid sound.

Her tongue thrashed against his. Her breasts quivered. Her hips undulated madly. And when he slid a second finger inside to join the first one, she momentarily stopped breathing.

Her entire body stiffened. He felt her hover on the edge, her muscles taut, straining. When he touched his thumb to her clitoris she let loose a high, keening sound of pleasure.

"Don't...stop," she begged, her voice muffled with the expectation of climax. "Oh, oh, oh..."

And then, in one shattering moment, she came.

Her muscles spasmed around his fingers, her buttocks arching off the sofa cushions. He'd never witnessed anything so lovely.

An indescribable emotion tightened his chest. He felt as much satisfaction as if he himself had climaxed. This was his purpose—to pleasure this beautiful woman and help her heal whatever demons it was that pursued her. For he knew without knowing how he'd come by the knowledge that she had followed him into the forest as a tonic for what ailed her. He was so happy that he had been able to give her this small respite.

She sagged against him and he held her close. He murmured sweet nothings in made-up Spanish, listened as her heart slowed from a racing gallop to a sedate pace.

He felt oddly sated, to the point that when she reached up in the darkness, cupped his chin and said, "Now it's your turn." He shook his head.

"No," he said softly.

She pushed against his chest, struggling to sit up. "Why not?" she asked.

Caleb frowned. It had been bugging him for a while now, ever since she'd forgotten to speak in her Klondike Kate vernacular. Her voice sounded naggingly familiar. Did he know her?

"I would rather wait."

He realized it was true. He had to see her again, and he feared if they fully consummated their passion he never would. But if he left her aching for more...who knew how long this game might last? Maybe, just maybe, she'd want to return for seconds.

"Wait?" Panic settled in her voice, obscuring the familiarity. "Wait for what? I don't want to wait."

He had her exactly where he wanted her. Caleb reached for her hand and held it tightly in his, even though she tried to pull back.

Eventually the throbbing in his groin would abate. Eventually.

"I want to see you again," he told her.

"No," she said adamantly, reverting back to her Klondike Kate drawl. "This is supposed to be a one-night stand. Now take your pants off."

"Relax. There's nothing to be afraid of."

"You don't understand. I don't want anything more from you than sex."

"I'm not saying I do, either," he cajoled, but his stomach pitched. Truth be told, he would like to see where this attraction might lead. See if the powerful sexual pull might take them to something deeper, more meaningful. "But I think dragging out the seduction will make it so much more memorable when we finally do go all the way."

Her nails bit into his palms. "It's not such a good idea."

"Why not?"

"Tonight we were overcome—by hormones, the

full moon, by our costumes. It was magical, special. Why ruin it? Just make love to me now so things aren't lopsided, and then I'll slip away into the darkness. Let's leave this a wonderful flight of fancy."

"I can't accept that."

What was the matter with him? What she was proposing was every guy's wildest fantasy. Anonymous sex with a beautiful stranger. No strings attached. No consequences. No regrets. Except more than anything in the world, he wanted to see her again. He was taking a risk, pressuring her like this, and he knew it, but he felt it was a risk worth taking.

"I must see you again," he insisted, unable to quell the urgency building inside him. "I must know more about you."

"Impossible."

"But why?" Then he froze as an ugly suspicion dawned. "Are you married?"

"No."

Caleb exhaled in relief. Thank heavens. He wasn't a home wrecker. "Then why deny us this pleasure?"

"Simple logistics, my dear Don Juan. I'm leaving town tomorrow morning."

"You're not from Bear Creek then?"

"No."

"I'm sorry, but I cannot let you get away." Stubbornly, he clung to her hand.

"Please, Don Juan, this was nothing more than an extravagant game. We both got turned on, but it's no more than that. Please, let it go."

"It's more than a game and you know it."

"It's not," she insisted.

"All right then," he said, scrambling for something

he could say that would change her mind. "Let me help you get dressed and I'll walk you back to the party."

Several minutes later, they were clothed again and walking through the forest hand in hand. His body was still stiff from wanting her. His mind raced with ways to convince her to see him a second time. Things couldn't end on this disappointing note.

Caleb led her into a moonlit field not far from the community center where the party still continued. Laughter, music, the sound of car doors slamming echoed in the still of the night.

He stopped, drew her closer to him and stared into that unfathomable face hidden so dramatically behind the red-feathered mask.

"What if I happened to come to where you lived? I travel a lot on business," he lied, still speaking in his Don Juan accent, reluctant to release the disguise and break the enchantment. "Could I see you then?"

She paused for a long moment. "Perhaps. I don't know."

His heart leaped with hope. "You realize this was special. How often have you felt this way?"

She inhaled deeply. "I'm not sure this is such a good idea."

"Think of all the fun we could have."

"Do you swear that it would only be fun? Nothing else? I don't want anything else."

"Nothing else," he promised. At this point he would promise her anything to get her phone number.

"I'm doing this against my better judgment, but you're right," she said. "I've never felt anything like what happened between us tonight. You've made me feel like a desirable woman.''

He made a deep sound of approval. ''You *are* a desirable woman.''

''Okay.'' She swallowed audibly. ''Here's the deal. I'll whisper my phone number to you and if you can remember it, then you can call me.''

Caleb's pulse pounded in his ears. He was beset by the riddle of her. He wanted her so badly it hurt. Wanted to be inside her, buried deep.

''Sweetheart, I could never forget,'' he crooned, meaning every word.

She whispered the number.

''What?'' Startled, he shook his head, certain he had heard incorrectly. ''Please say that one more time.''

She repeated herself.

With the rapidity of lightning striking, his blood froze. His world skidded to a screeching halt. His ears echoed with the sound of her voice mouthing those digits. Realization dawned. He knew that number. Had called it many times over the years.

''Good night,'' she whispered. ''And if I never see you again, goodbye. I'll always remember the precious gift you gave me in the skaters' cabin, Don Juan. Thank you.''

Then, without another word, she turned and started toward the community center, her graceful body illuminated in moon glow.

He literally could not speak. His senses reeled. He splayed a palm over his heart. He knew now who she was. No wonder she had sounded familiar. No wonder he had been so inexplicably attracted to her.

She was the woman who had dominated his teenage fantasies. The very same woman who had once been married to his stepbrother Jesse.

Klondike Kate, the lady upon whom he'd just performed sexual maneuvers, was none other than his unrequited childhood crush.

Meggie Scofield.

5

"HOT DAMN, woman. I love the hair!" Wendy Roseneau, Meggie's next-door neighbor and good friend for the past five years, declared.

It was three days after her return home to Seattle. Wendy, a brown-eyed, bottle blonde with Kewpie doll cheeks and a Cindy Crawford beauty mark over her upper lip, settled her hands on her hips and nodded approvingly as Vincent, a tattooed, nose-pierced, fuchsia-haired stylist at En Avant!, the trendiest salon in Seattle, put the finishing touches on Meggie's dashing new coif.

"Your friend's right, darling. You look absolutely plucky," Vincent enthused.

Plucky? Her?

Sure. Why not? Yes, by gosh. Her. Plucky.

"You were in desperate need of a change," Vincent continued, waving his hand with a theatrical flourish. "That bland Buster Brown blunt cut you were sporting was just too, too retro. I'm sooo glad you chose me to be the artist of your transformation. You are my masterpiece, my muse, my Mona Lisa."

Okay, so Vincent was a bit of a drama queen but he did have a point. The conversion was startling.

Meggie stared into the mirror. The difference in her appearance astounded her. The spiky cut flipped out from her head in short, sassy wisps. The style not only slimmed her face and accentuated her green eyes but also lent her a hip, dynamic edge.

She looked like the kind of woman who took life full throttle. It was exactly what she'd been seeking when she'd plunked herself in Vincent's chair and asked him to create a wild, new, independent persona for her.

"Wow," she murmured and reached up to lightly finger her hair. "Wow."

"Wow indeed," Wendy concurred. "You should have gotten divorced years ago. Freedom definitely agrees with you."

"It's not just the divorce," Meggie whispered to Wendy as she slipped Vincent a tip so big he actually purred.

Normally, she wasn't the kind of woman to kiss and tell, but she was filled to the bursting with thoughts of her erotic night with Don Juan.

"Oh no?" Wendy rubbed her hands gleefully. "I smell a juicy story. What's up?"

"Come on. I'll tell you later. In the meantime I'm buying a whole new wardrobe at La Chic Freak."

Wendy plastered a hand over her heart. "You? In La Chic Freak?"

"Yep. I'm going for leather and lace and chains. And who knows? Maybe I'll even get a henna tattoo."

"Omigosh, I thought I'd never live to see the day you decided to recognize your full potential and rebel against that good-girl image that's kept you trapped in that tight little black-and-white box. I'm so proud of you, Megs.'' Wendy wrapped her in a honeysuckle-scented hug.

''Me, too,'' Vincent chimed in. ''You go, girlfriend.''

Geez. She knew she'd been something of fuddy-duddy but she had no idea everyone had been holding their breath just waiting for her to cut loose. This had certainly been a week of prolonged self-discovery.

And it's all because you stepped outside your comfort zone and took a gamble.

The evening she'd spent in the skaters' cabin with Don Juan had been the most liberating experience of her life. Ever since that fateful night she felt changed in ways she couldn't explain. Ways that made her long for all the things she'd missed. Why had she hidden her light under a bushel all these years?

Well, no more. From now on, everything was going to be different.

She and Wendy left the salon and headed for La Chic Freak. An hour later she emerged wearing a red mesh blouse and a matching red leather miniskirt so short it would have caused even Klondike Kate to blush. In her hands swung a shopping bag filled with equally intrepid clothing.

''Okay,'' Wendy said as they wandered down the street. ''We're out of earshot of anyone. Spill it. What in the world happened to you in Alaska?''

She tried not to smirk, but couldn't help herself. ''I met the most awesome guy.''

''Get out!''

''It's true.''

Wendy stopped walking and smacked her forehead with a palm. ''No, no, no. Please say it ain't so.''

"What?" Meggie felt perplexed. "I thought you would be happy that I met someone."

"Yes, in a year or so. Maybe. Not yet. It's too soon after your divorce, sweetie."

"I've been divorced for six months."

"No good can come of this relationship. He's nothing but the transition guy. A temporary fix. You need to live a little before you get involved with anyone else."

"Give me some credit, will you? I totally realize that. Why do you think I got this new haircut and bought new outfits? Believe me, this thing with Don Juan was nothing but a fling."

"Don Juan? Oh, please tell me you're kidding."

"Settle down. Don Juan's not his real name and, besides, I'm never going to see him again."

"You? A one-night stand?" Wendy shook her head, incredulous. "Not that there's anything wrong with a good, lusty romp in the hay once in a while, but I just never thought you of all people..."

"Not only that," Meggie whispered. "I don't even know his real name."

"What?"

Leaving out the most intimate details, Meggie told Wendy about Don Juan, the costume party and the cabin in the woods.

"From what you describe it sounds like there was a whole lot of sexual chemistry going on," Wendy said when Meggie had finished. "That kind of passion can be hard to ignore, particularly with a guy who has obviously made you feel special. I have been there and I've been burned. Be careful, sweetie. I'd hate to see you get hurt."

"Don't worry. He doesn't know my name, either. We were two ships passing in the night."

"Well," Wendy said, linking her arm through Meggie's and continuing down the street to where they'd parked the car, "maybe you're right. Maybe this was exactly what you needed. I certainly approve of the changes in you."

"Honestly, I swear, it's just what the doctor ordered. I've never felt so free. It's like I've unearthed this confidence in myself I didn't even know I had."

"And you promise you're never going to see this guy again?"

"I promise." Meggie held up two fingers. "Girl Scouts' honor."

"That's good. As long as you're not tempted to jump into a relationship with a man you don't know just because the sex is stupendous."

"Absolutely not."

"Then congratulations on stretching the limits of your imagination."

"Thank you," Meggie said, but a nagging little voice reminded her that she wasn't being completely honest with her friend. She *had* given Don Juan her telephone number.

But what were the chances of him even remembering her number? And if he did remember it, what were the odds of him calling her or ever coming to Seattle to see her?

Very slim to none. She was safe with her lusty memories. She didn't have to worry about falling hard for some stranger in a black leather mask. All Meggie cared about was exploring her newfound sense of adventure in whatever form it might take. New hairstyle, new clothes, new experiences.

And speaking of new experiences…

She stopped in front of the dance studio sandwiched between La Chic Freak and En Avant! Through the window she spied a group of costumed belly dancers executing a series of mesmerizing gyrations.

For the longest time she had hankered to take belly dancing lessons, but because Jesse had called her an awkward klutz the time she had tried to do a striptease for him, Meggie had felt too self-conscious about her body to give belly dancing a go.

Well, phooey on her ex and his stupid opinions. Thanks to Don Juan she was more than eager to rip the envelope of adventure wide open.

Purposefully, she pushed through the door of the dance studio.

"Hey," Wendy said. "Where you are going?"

Meggie glanced over her shoulder at her friend and grinned. "To stretch the limits of my imagination."

"MAY I SPEAK TO YOU in my office?" Meggie's boss, Jenny Arbenoit, asked three weeks after her shopping spree with Wendy.

"Sure," Meggie said, wondering what was up.

She didn't think she'd made any mistakes lately, but perhaps she had gone overboard with her newfound confidence. Recently, she had stopped kowtowing to the doctors' every whim, and she'd also started making more decisions based on her own assessments without asking for corroboration from her colleagues as she once had. A sinking sensation settled in her stomach.

It was a slow afternoon in the emergency department. The nurses had been enjoying a welcome respite from earlier in the week, when they'd been deluged with nearly an epidemic of children suffering from high fevers related to a recent outbreak of a Lyme disease type illness. Meggie had been catching up on paperwork when Jenny singled her out.

Mouth dry, and prepared to offer an apology, she followed Jenny into her office.

"Have a seat." Her boss indicated a chair and closed the door behind them.

Meggie sat and nervously eyed the older woman.

"Meggie, ever since you returned from your leave of absence, I've noticed a change in you."

"Mrs. Arbenoit, if I've done anything—"

Jenny held up her hand. "Please, let me finish. Several of your co-workers have also commented on your new attitude. You've always been a good nurse—kind, caring, considerate of others—but until these last few weeks you have lacked the kind of self-confidence that would make you management material."

"Excuse me?"

"Your exemplary performance during this latest public health crisis has not gone unnoticed by the doctors. You've assumed more responsibility and presented yourself as a thorough professional."

Meggie's head spun. She wasn't being taken to task. She was being praised.

"We were hoping you would accept a position on

the community health education board. Do you think this is something that might interest you?"

"Absolutely." Ideas sprouted in her head. She loved teaching patients, and this was a marvelous opportunity to boost her career.

"Excellent, excellent." Jenny Arbenoit got to her feet and extended her hand. "I'm looking forward to working on the board with you."

"Thanks." Meggie shook her hand, a sense of pride filling her chest. A new job offer because of her increased self-confidence. Just one more debt of gratitude she owed to Don Juan.

CALEB STARED OUT the window of the ranger station at the vast white expanse of new-fallen snow. It had been six weeks since that fateful night he'd discovered his new lover was none other than his teenage fantasy woman. Six weeks since his world had been turned completely upside down. For the first time in his life, the wilderness he loved so deeply felt desolate and lonely.

With Meggie gone, everything in his world seemed quiet, dull, empty. He got through his daily routine, but nothing brought him joy. Listlessly, he dug in the pocket of his crisp, hunter-green uniform shirt and pulled out a photograph he'd gleaned from an old album—a picture Jesse had taken of him and Meggie together on the rare occasion he'd visited them in Seattle.

It had been Christmas Eve. He and Meggie were sitting on the couch together. He had on a Santa hat, and she wore a blue package bow stuck in her hair. They'd had too much holiday eggnog, and Meggie, with one arm thrown over his shoulder, was mugging cutely for the camera. He'd been staring at her with a look of such deep admiration it was a wonder neither Jesse nor Meggie had ever noticed. Hell, even Caleb had never realized before how much like a lovesick puppy he looked.

And he'd told himself he'd gotten over his childhood crush. Ha! One glance at the photo and he knew he'd been lying to himself for years.

The photograph was frayed now, the edges curled from wear. As he did every day since discovering Klondike Kate was actually Meggie, he traced a finger over the picture and murmured her name.

He recalled how she'd looked the last time he'd seen her, dressed in that scarlet bustier and auburn wig. He thought of her sweet scent, and his imagination supplied the aroma he was searching for—jasmine soap, strawberry shampoo and a hint of Obsession cologne.

His brain didn't stop with scent memories. He thought about those cinnamon freckles that decorated her collarbone and those intelligent green eyes the color of verdant summer grass. He envisioned her soft, womanly curves, the creamy taste of her full, rich lips and the way she'd felt wrapped in his arms. The way her body had responded to his touch.

In a twinkling, he was transported back to that astounding night.

Slowly, tenderly, he removes her red-feathered mask and the long auburn wig in order to reveal her own coal-black hair. She does not resist. She is not ashamed to let him see her face. And when he removes his mask, she is not alarmed or upset. He sucks in his breath, overwhelmed. His heart thumps at her easy acceptance of his role as her lover.

She wants him. In fact, she lifts her arms to him and a tempting smile teases her lips as she slowly undoes the top hook of her bustier.

Another tiny hook undone. Another and then another, until the stiff lacy material lays open just beneath the swell of her breasts. The cool evening breeze causes her nipples to tighten into pink pouting buds.

Her eyelids drift closed. Loose tendrils of dark hair curl invitingly over her forehead. Her lips part. She tips her chin up.

"Kiss me," she commands.

His blood is at the boiling point, and he's clutched so hard with need he doesn't know if he'll be able to control himself.

But he must. For her sake. No matter how much his body aches for a frenzied coupling, he will not surrender to the instincts raging within. Not yet.

Apparently, however, she is feeling just as desperate as he, for she opens her eyes, takes hold of his shirt in her fists and rips the garment from his body. She splays her palms against his chest and then savagely sinks her nails into his flesh. Her breath hisses out through clenched teeth in a sultry sizzle.

His bulge is straining hard against his leather pants. Roughly, he grasps her wrists and pins her hands above her head.

"Is this how you want it? Fast and hard?"

In answer, she just growls and raises her head to nip at his throat.

He claims her mouth with a merciless kiss that

leaves them both gasping for air. He glides his fingertips down her raised arms to her exposed breasts. She shivers at his featherlight touch, obviously confused, but also delighted by his change in tactics.

Using great care, he unhooks her bustier completely and pushes it open until her flat, ivory-white stomach is bare. He makes quick work of the tap pants, shoving them past her hips. The delicate wisp of red satin tangles around her ankles. She helps, kicking the panties off into the darkness.

Restlessly, she undulates her hips, calling him back down to her. When he lowers his head and takes one of her pert nipples into his mouth, a low guttural moan slips from her lips.

He caresses his hands along the smooth, firm planes of her body, exploring every inch of her. She is any man's dream lover. The fantasy woman to end all fantasies, and at long last, she is his.

He wants her so badly he can barely think, but at the same time, he wants to draw this night out and make it last forever.

Cupping her hips in his palms, he lifts her up and she gyrates against his erection.

“Take off the pants,” she commands. “Now. I want to see you. Touch you. Taste you.”

At the notion of her tasting his shaft, he almost comes right then and there.

Control. Hold on to your control.

But how impossible this wonderful woman was making that task. She was actively licking his chest while he fumbled with the drawstrings of his pants.

Then he was naked, his pants flung out into the

empty cabin, and her fingers—oh, her wicked fingers—were wrapping around his hard cock.

"I've spent my life waiting for you," she whispers. "Take me, Caleb. Make me your own."

"Mail call!" Quinn Scofield's booming voice, and the loud thumping of his feet on the staircase, yanked Caleb from his X-rated reverie.

Cricket on a crutch! He'd been fantasizing about his best friend's baby sister, and now here was Quinn, coming through his front door.

Caleb tossed the Christmas photograph aside, grabbed the high-powered field binoculars from the table and pulled them into his lap to disguise the vestige of his arousal.

"Hey, Greenleaf." Quinn came grinning into the cabin, stomping snow off his boots and bringing the cold, late-October air with him. "What's happening?"

If only you knew, you'd probably punch my lights out.

"Morning, Scofield. You didn't have to make a trip up here. I was headed into Bear Creek tomorrow to pick up supplies."

Quinn dumped the mail onto the table. "Truth is, buddy, we were all a little worried about you. I know you're the strong, silent type, but we've hardy seen you in town since the *Metropolitan* party."

"No need to worry about me. I'm just tired of the matchmaking and having women throw themselves at me. It's getting harder and harder to tell the sincere ones from the gold diggers."

"Old Gus commented that you might have a harder

time finding an honest woman because of your money.''

''Don't you people have anything better to do than gossip about me?''

''As the last remaining bachelor, Greenleaf, you're a cause for much speculation.''

''Lucky me. Let me guess—old Gus has got a pool going about my future marital status.''

Quinn's grin was answer enough.

Caleb shook his head. ''So what's your bet?''

''I'm predicting you'll be swept off your feet by the pretty interim park ranger who takes your place while you're in Seattle. You'll get married here in the ranger station next summer—I forecast a June wedding—have sixteen kids and live happily ever after.''

''What are you talking about? I'm not going to Seattle.''

But even as he denied this statement, Caleb's heart rate accelerated. There was no way Quinn could know he'd spent the past six weeks debating whether or not to go to Seattle after Meggie.

Quinn reached in the mail sack, withdrew a letter and passed it over to Caleb.

''Have you been reading my mail?'' He frowned.

''Didn't have to. Talked to Meggie this morning.''

''Meggie?''

''You know, my sister. Your ex-stepsister-in-law.''

''I know who she is. What does her calling you have to do with me going to Seattle?'' His gut twisted with a mix of excitement and hope.

''Read the letter.''

Caleb stared down at the return address of King

County Health Department, Seattle, Washington, then flipped the envelope over and opened the flap.

The letter was from the director of public health services. There had been a massive outbreak of a tick-born illness in Seattle and the surrounding counties. The ailment mimicked Lyme disease. The local medical community was woefully lacking in knowledge about the type of ticks that caused the condition. They needed an expert to come to Seattle, all expenses paid, and give a series of lectures at area hospitals for the next four weeks. Caleb's name had been recommended by one of the board members, Meggie Scofield. The director had worked out a deal with the park services of Alaska. In exchange for Caleb coming to Seattle, one of Washington's naturalists would take his place in the Tongass during his absence.

It was the perfect excuse to go to Seattle. At the thought of seeing Meggie again, Caleb's chest squeezed.

He had to remind himself this meant nothing. Meggie didn't know he was Don Juan. She had suggested his name to her superiors simply because he knew more about insects than anyone in the Pacific Northwest, not because she secretly wanted to see him again.

Unless something on a subconscious level was at work here. He looked over at Quinn. "Meggie recommended me?"

"Sure. Why not? You are the best bug guy around. She's on the board. In fact, she's on the committee that's throwing a Halloween charity ball to raise money for public awareness of Lyme disease and other tick-born illnesses. If you take the job, maybe you'll be in time to attend.''

Caleb pushed the envelope away. Apprehension took hold of him. What if he did go to Seattle, tell Meggie he was Don Juan, and she rejected him?

''I don't know. A month is a long time to be away.''

''Come on, Greenleaf. You need to get out of the forest every once in a while, and you said yourself you're tired of all these women throwing themselves at you. No one in Seattle except Meggie will know you're a millionaire bachelor. Take off—have a good time.''

''I suppose it would be a vacation of sorts.''

''Darn right. Go for it, man. Get Meggie to show you around town and introduce you to some of her cute single girlfriends.''

''I thought I was suppose to fall in love with the interim ranger and have sixteen kids.''

''Come on, everyone needs a plan B. What if the interim ranger is a guy?''

''Good point.''

Caleb thought of the Don Juan costume stuffed in the top of his closet. A Halloween party charity event put on by Meggie's hospital. He could show up a few days early, take the costume with him to Seattle, wear it to the party, and then he could take off the mask and show her face-to-face that he was the man who'd enflamed her that night in the forest.

Take a gamble. Roll the dice. Go to Seattle.

He had nothing to lose.

Nothing, that is, except his heart.

6

"SO TELL ME MORE ABOUT this cute, rich friend of yours giving the symposiums."

"Caleb?" Meggie glanced over at Wendy.

"You got more than one cute, rich, lecture-giving friend?"

"No." Meggie chuckled. "Just Caleb."

They were taking their daily jog around the park adjacent to their downtown apartment complex. A foggy mist had settled on trees resplendent with a vivid splash of autumn color, dampening the ground and lending a slight chill to the air.

"Caleb." Wendy rolled his name on her tongue. "I like it. Sounds rugged and woodsy and he-mannish."

"He is."

"Ooh." She gave a little shiver of delight that for some unknown reason irritated Meggie. "Tell me more. What's he like?"

"He's really not your type."

"What's that suppose to mean?" Wendy slowed, but Meggie kept going.

"You're a party girl," she called over her shoulder.

"And?"

"You'll spend a month's salary on a pair of Manolo Blahniks."

"So?"

"Caleb lives in a park ranger station in the middle of the Tongass National Forest, Wendy. He uses a two-way radio for a telephone. Not too many occasions turn up for putting on the Ritz."

"Hey, wait up! I'm falling behind," Wendy hollered, but Meggie never slowed her pace.

Why should she care who Caleb went out with? Besides, the guy needed a little fun in his life. He was much too serious, and if anyone could lighten him up, effervescent Wendy could do the trick.

You feel protective toward him. He's practically like a brother. You don't want to see him get hurt, that's all, Meggie reassured herself. Her feelings for Caleb were strictly platonic.

Then why are you feeling jealous? a tiny voice in the back of her head whispered. But she ignored the obnoxious nudge. Meggie had enough trouble dealing with this obsession she'd developed for Don Juan without throwing Caleb Greenleaf into the mix.

What was wrong with her, anyway? Why couldn't she forget about Don Juan? She knew he wasn't good for her, and yet night after night she had hauntingly erotic dreams about the masked man coming to her bed and making fierce, passionate love to her.

Probably because he had curtailed their sexual adventure that night in the cabin. Meggie felt certain if they had consummated their romantic assignation she would not be fixated on him. It was a clear case of wanting what she couldn't have.

Wendy, panting and red-faced, finally caught up with her. "Witch. Why didn't you slow down?"

"Interval training. You burn more calories this

way,'' Meggie said, slowing at last and feeling a bit ashamed of herself for sprinting ahead. She reduced her speed to a fast walk, and Wendy shot her a grateful smile.

''So about Caleb…''

Obviously, her friend wasn't going to let go of the subject. Meggie sighed. ''Yes?''

''What's he like?''

''Tall, dark hair, deep-blue eyes, handsome as a Greek statue.''

''Yum, tell me more.''

''He's quiet, somber, deeply into nature and very intelligent. That's why I recommended him as a lecturer. Actually, I'm pretty surprised he accepted. He generally hates to leave Alaska.''

''The strong, silent type.'' Wendy licked her lips. ''I'm intrigued.''

''He's a great guy.'' Meggie gazed across the street at a schoolyard where a group of kids played soccer. Why watching those kids at play should make her feel wistful, she had no idea. Maybe because she was beginning to wonder if she'd ever have any kids of her own. ''A good listener. But you would probably think he was boring.''

''Hmm.'' Wendy stopped walking.

Meggie halted. ''Hmm, what?''

''Why don't you want me to go out with him?''

''I never said that.''

''Come on, you tell me how great he is on the one hand but warn me off on the other. Saving him for yourself, are you? That's a little selfish, considering your almost religiouslike conversion after your naughty costumed tryst with the suave Don Juan.''

"Don't be silly. I'm not interested in Caleb."

"Why not? He sounds perfect."

"For one thing, he's younger than I am."

"Oh, big deal." Wendy waved a hand.

"And he's Jesse's stepbrother."

Wendy made a face. "I can see where that could cause problems, but still..."

"He loves Alaska, and I love Seattle."

"True love conquers all."

"I just don't have *those* kinds of feelings for him."

"Okay then. Since we got that cleared up, you gotta introduce him to me."

Meggie swallowed. She wasn't sure Caleb would appreciate being fixed up, but Wendy was a lot of fun to be around. Even if she and Caleb didn't click, maybe they could at least have a good time together.

"All right. I'll introduce you."

"Hot dog!" Wendy did a little jig, and then gave Meggie a hug. "A decent date prospect for the first time in weeks. Megs, you're a doll."

Yeah. But how was Caleb going to take the news?

THE MINUTE HIS PLANE touched down at SeaTac Airport, Caleb remembered why he didn't like big cities.

Crowds. Noise. Traffic congestion. Pollution.

He'd been to Seattle only once before and he'd had the same reaction. The frantic pace gave him a headache. Hurry, hurry. Where was everyone dashing off to in such an all-fired rush?

It took him a good forty-five minutes to find the baggage claim terminal and retrieve his luggage. Then another ten minutes wading through the jostling throng to find the taxi stand.

Feeling like a stranger in a strange land, he suspected the cabbie was driving him around in circles, but he had no proof. When the guy pulled up in front of his hotel and told him the fare was thirty-six dollars, his suspicions were confirmed.

He tried arguing, but the driver suddenly pretended he didn't speak English. Grudgingly, Caleb paid the fare, but as he turned to deliver his bags to the bellhop, a scruffy-looking teen on a bicycle darted up the hotel's circular drive, leaned down and scooped up his briefcase. The kid disappeared before Caleb realized what had happened.

Dammit!

All the notes for his lecture were in that briefcase. Stupid kid was going to be disappointed when he pried open the case and discovered it contained nothing more than a treatise on ticks and half a power bar.

An hour later, after a powwow with hotel security and a Seattle police officer who was not optimistic about Caleb's ever seeing his briefcase again, he was finally ensconced in his room.

If it wasn't for Meggie, he would have been sorely tempted to turn around and head straight back to Bear Creek. But she had staked her reputation on him, recommending him as a guest lecturer. He wasn't going to let her down. Even if he would have to wing his speech.

Besides, how could he leave Seattle without seeing her again? At the very notion of meeting up with her his heart went *thumpa-thumpa-thumpa.*

Call her. Let her know you got a lower fare by coming in on Friday night instead of Sunday, a little voice whispered.

Caleb circled the phone. ''Go ahead, Greenleaf. Call her.''

Determined, he perched on the edge of the bed, reached for the telephone and punched in her number.

It rang three times and he almost hung up.

''Hello.''

Meggie's voice was so breathy, so overwhelmingly sexy, he sat stunned for a good ten seconds, his fingers wrapped tightly around the receiver.

''Hello?'' she repeated.

Heat, sultry and sudden, swamped his body. How he wanted her!

Caleb opened his mouth to say, ''Hi Megs, it's me. I just got into town,'' but instead it seemed as if alien forces captured his throat and took possession of his larynx. He'd never in a million years intended on saying what he said next.

''*Buenos dias,* belladonna,'' he crooned in Don Juan's husky accent. ''Are you surprised to hear from me?''

MEGGIE ALMOST DROPPED the receiver as her stomach slid into her sensible bedroom slippers.

Oh dear, oh dear, oh dear.

She plastered a palm against her bare chest above where her towel covered her breasts. She had just stepped out of the shower, following her jog with Wendy, when the telephone rang.

Water from her wet hair trickled down her back. She heard the distant whizzing of cars on the freeway. Tasted the tangy flavor of her own desire on the tip of her tongue.

For the past six-and-a-half weeks she had scarcely

thought of anything besides that magical night with Don Juan when she'd dared to let go of her inhibitions and had discovered a whole new side of herself.

Meggie Scofield could be as wild and wanton as the next girl.

Her pulse was pounding a rhythmic tyranny. She hadn't really expected him to come to Seattle, or even call her, for that matter.

Meggie's knees loosened. She groped for one of the straight-back chairs gathered around the kitchen table, and sat down hard.

"Don Juan?" she whispered.

"Do you have any other Spanish lovers?"

Ripples of desire undulated up her spine. What was it about the man that caused such sensations to engulf her?

"I have been unable to forget you."

She heard the sly smile in his voice, felt a corresponding hitch in her belly. She laughed as much to dispel the strange achiness inside her than anything else.

"You're a little hard to forget yourself."

"So it was not my imagination. You felt for me the same as I felt for you." His rich masculine sound wrapped around her like a blanket.

"It wasn't your imagination," she murmured, having no idea why she said that. What in the heck did she want from him? What did she think she was doing?

"I dream about you day and night. Night and day."

"Oh?" She forced herself to sound cool, casual.

"Yes. I think of the way you move, so graceful, like a swan skimming over a peaceful lake."

It was corny and hokey and blatantly a line but, heaven help her, she was falling for it. With shaky fingers, she shoved a spike of soppy hair behind her ear.

"Your walk is so sensuous. Perhaps because you have such beautiful legs. The shape of them, so slender and feminine, excites me beyond measure."

"Really?"

She was a weak, weak woman. The man was no good for her and she knew it. She should hang up the phone on him right now and forget he'd ever called.

But she did not.

"Your legs and your butt excite me."

"My butt?" His use of frank language both startled her and turned her on.

"Yes, you possess a fine bottom. Nothing inflames a man more than a woman with a narrow waist and generous hips."

He thought her big rear end was sexy? Pensively, Meggie reached around and patted her fanny.

"If I were there with you right now, I would pinch your butt. Not too hard, just enough to let you know how much I admire it."

Hang up! Hang up!

Meggie cleared her throat. "Then what?"

His chuckle was smooth and seductive. "Ah."

"What's that suppose to mean?"

"You know what it means."

"I don't."

"But you do."

What was he insinuating? That he wanted to have phone sex with her? She'd never talked dirty over the telephone and she wasn't about to start now.

Prude.

I'm not, Meggie silently insisted.

Prove it. Step outside the box.

"What are you wearing?" he asked.

She glanced down at the beach towel wrapped around her midsection and winced. Think dowdy. Stop this before it gets started.

"A sweatsuit," she lied.

"I do not believe you."

"Okay, what do you think I'm wearing?"

Dammit, Meggie, why did you say that?

"I think perhaps you are wearing baby doll pajamas. Or maybe a silky, sheer black negligee."

Meggie laughed.

"Or maybe..." His voice, already deep, dropped another octave "...you're wearing nothing at all."

Whew, that was too close for comfort.

"But I hope you are wearing something," he continued. "Because I'd like to imagine undressing you. I'd like to slowly slide those skinny black negligee straps off your shoulders."

"Umm."

"I wish I could kiss you," he said. "Would you like that?"

Unbidden, she imagined Don Juan there with her, nibbling her lips, his tongue gliding over her mouth. She realized then she was panting in short, fevered gasps.

"Yes," she murmured helplessly, "yes."

"And then I would like to run my hot tongue over your gorgeous bare breasts."

She sucked in her breath and unknotted the towel.

"Stroke yourself. Pretend I am there. That it is my fingers touching you. Remember what it felt like?"

She did as he commanded, rubbing her nipples and delighting in the erotic sensation.

"Does that feel good?"

"Yes," she gasped.

"I wish I could lick you. Kiss you. Hold you. I'm getting hard just thinking about you."

"I'm getting excited, too," she panted, thrashing about in the chair as she ran her hands down her belly to the triangle of hair between her legs.

"I wish I could slip my hands into your panties and stroke your warm, wet..." He spoke a word that made her blush and ache to come all at the same time.

Perspiration beaded on her forehead as her brain spiraled off into another seductively vivid scenario. She imagined him sliding her naked body down the length of his until she was on her knees, her lips even with the hard length of his erection. She envisioned wrapping her warm, moist mouth around his manhood until he groaned with ecstasy and begged for mercy.

She saw herself pinned under his hard, masculine body, his manly fingers tangling in her hair, holding her prisoner while he ravished her with his mouth, feasting on her nipples, dragging his tongue along her belly, then lower to her heated depths.

A sharp shudder thrust its way through Meggie's system and she shifted in her seat, crossing one leg over the other in a desperate attempt to stay the sensations flooding her groin.

"I count the moments until I see you again," he whispered. "Until I can kiss you and gaze into your beautiful green eyes."

Absently, she ran a hand along her throat, fingered the erratic pulse beating there and was surprised to find her skin so warm to the touch. Desire heated her from the inside out and made her crave this man's presence.

"I must see you again." His voice through the phone line was a low, masculine rumble of urgent sound that grabbed hold of her and aroused the most secret places of her body.

"I'd like to see you, too."

"To finish what we started."

She felt her face flush hot, but, yes, this was what she wanted, what she had dreamed of for the past seven weeks.

"Yes," she murmured softly.

"I will be arriving in Seattle in the morning. I have business to attend to during the day, but my evening is reserved for you."

"I can't tomorrow night. I'm attending a Halloween charity event."

"I'm only in town for one night. I must see you tomorrow or not at all."

He was pressuring her, but damn if she didn't want to see him again. "You may come to the Halloween party if you like. If you've got a pen, I can give you the name and address of the hotel where it's being held."

"Should I come as Don Juan?"

"But of course."

A thrill ran through her at the mental picture of his tight leather pants and shiny black boots. She certainly did not want him to come without a costume. If she was going to have a red-hot, mindless affair with this man, she must not know his real name or see the face behind the mask.

She bit down on her bottom lip. Molten passion seeped through her being with a heat that obscured all rational thought.

"Are you there?" he asked, his devastating accent fueling the fire between her legs. "Are you all right?"

Meggie blinked and realized several seconds had gone by while she had indulged her fantasies. She cleared her throat.

"Fine. I'm fine."

"Until tomorrow night," he whispered.

"Until tomorrow night," Meggie echoed, not knowing how she was going to make it through the next twenty-four hours.

CALEB HAD STUNNED HIMSELF. He couldn't believe he had said those provocative things to her over the telephone. And after he'd hung up, alone in his hotel room with nothing but erotic visions of Meggie pleasuring herself, he had been forced to take matters into his own hands. There was only so much control a guy could command before the dam burst.

Now here he was, dressed as Don Juan, in a taxi on the way to the Halloween party. His blood surged feverishly with thoughts of the night ahead. How and when was he going to reveal himself to Meggie?

While he was enjoying this masquerade, he couldn't keep it up forever. And dammit, call it ego, but he was ready for her to know that he, the guy she considered no more than a friend, was the one pushing her sexual buttons.

But he also knew that Meggie was loving this game

they'd built, and wearing a disguise was what gave her confidence to move into uncharted territory, just as the Don Juan costume supplied him with the courage to take a chance on fulfilling his fantasies.

He smiled to himself. Meggie Scofield. What a woman! Brave and smart and sexy as hell.

The taxi parked in front of the Claremont Hotel. Caleb paid the fare and got out. As he walked through the elegant, upscale European-style lobby, numerous feminine heads turned to stare in his direction.

He barely noticed. All his thoughts were concentrated on one woman and one woman only. In a brash move, he stopped at the front desk and made a room reservation for the night.

Are you sure this is such a smart thing to do? his practical side argued. *Aren't you assuming a lot? And what if you do make love to Meggie? What if it turns out to be terrible and you end up ruining your friendship?*

He thrust out his jaw and shoved aside the voice that kept him trodding the straight and narrow. Keeping quiet, holding back, had never gotten him what he wanted. The only time he'd achieved success was when he'd pursued something with passion.

When he crossed over into the packed ballroom, he realized he had no idea what costume Meggie would be wearing tonight. Feeling at a loss, he found a vantage point by the front entrance from which to peruse the crowd.

Suddenly, two hands slipped around his mask and covered his eyes, her dainty pinkies tickling his fake mustache. "Guess who."

Caleb started at the sound of her voice, so familiar

and melodious. He began to turn toward her, but a hand on his shoulder stilled him.

"Wait."

She was so close he could feel her soft breath fanning the nape of his neck, and despite the crowds in the ballroom, he felt as if they were totally and completely alone.

"Guess who," she repeated.

"I need a clue."

"Think extravagant."

"Well, that narrows it down."

"Someone sinfully rich."

"Don't tell me. Wait. I've got it. Bill Gates is flirting with me?"

Meggie's laugh sent an arrow of pure sexual energy shooting straight to his groin. "Not that rich and further back in history."

"Marie Antoinette."

"Closer, but not so headless."

The lush, velvety material of her sleeve scratched gently against his cheek. She rested her elbows on his shoulders and he could feel her breasts brushing seductively against his cape.

Alarmed, Caleb became cognizant of the very stunning effect this new game was having on the other parts of his body. He felt a swift stirring of arousal. If she didn't step away from him soon he was bound to embarrass them both.

"Guess who," she whispered into his ear again, her hands still locked in front of his face.

He'd never noticed before what cute palms she had, and her fingers were long and delicate. Refined. Certainly not the hands of an Alaskan woman. She belonged here, he realized with a twinge. In this city.

And he did not.

Before he could follow that depressing train of thought too far, Meggie did something that completely knocked him for a loop. She stood on tiptoe, leaned in close and ran her hot little tongue along this ear.

It was the most incredibly erotic thing anyone had ever done to him. He felt his control unraveling fast. What was she playing at?

"Come find me if you can," she whispered, then turned and disappeared into the crowd.

7

DRESSED AS Catherine the Great, Meggie slipped across the room and found a place to hunker down behind Dracula, the Wolf Man, Michael Jordan and John Wayne, who were discussing the pros and cons of extended antibiotic therapy in the long-term treatment of tick-born illnesses.

Her pulse was pumping with enough endorphins to kick start a Harley. She was high on adventure and the thrill of the chase. Crazed with a bright excitement as memorable as childhood Christmas mornings.

She certainly hadn't planned this little escapade. She'd simply spied Don Juan standing in the crowd and had gone to greet him, but by the time she'd made her way over, he had his back to her. Impulse had driven her to stand on tiptoe, rest her elbows on his shoulders and cover his eyes with her hands. Impulse and animal instinct.

His sharp intake of breath at her presence, his rich masculine scent, the way his broad shoulders had tensed beneath that silky white pirate shirt had compelled her to take things a step further. To dare him to figure out what disguise she was wearing and try to find her in the midst of the costumed congregation.

She should have known better. Hadn't that night in the forest taught her that hunting and capturing a mate was a compulsion written in a man's genetic code? By extending him this challenge, she'd effectively pitted herself against thousands of years of evolutionary conditioning.

And now Don Juan was on a quest, stalking through the gathered horde with a confident, ground-eating stride and an expression of serious intent riding his tightened jaw: he was searching for her.

What a buzz! What a lark! What a fantasy!

Meggie's mouth was dry, and she shivered from her head to her feet. She felt warm and jittery, as if she'd downed a half-dozen espressos in one sitting.

Was she losing control of the situation?

This masquerade was in danger of becoming an obsession. Don Juan made her feel things she had never felt before. Wonderful, delicious things she wanted to explore more fully.

Did she truly dare finish what they had started in the Tongass?

Dracula shifted to one side, leaving Meggie exposed to the crowd. She glanced around the room, looking for a new place to hide, but when she tilted her head to the right, there was Don Juan, standing just a few feet away, an inscrutable smile on his enigmatic lips.

The minute their eyes met Meggie knew she was in trouble. He started toward her. Meggie gulped. What was he going to do?

Wicked intent glistened in those commanding blue eyes, made even more powerful by the erotic frame of his black leather mask.

Her stomach fluttered. A jolt of pure, raw sexual

energy rushed through her and her world narrowed, shifted into agonizing slow motion.

Stomp, stomp, stomp. The noise of his boots striking the marble floor was sharpened and elongated, echoing loudly in her ears with each resounding step. His black hair was wildly tousled. The material of his silky shirt rippled when he walked, fluid as water. His gaze was locked on hers and she was helpless to look away, even to move. In what seemed both an eternity and a mere whisper of a second, he was at her side.

My God, he was handsome.

He reached out and wrapped a hand around her right elbow. The pressure of his fingers caused her to disintegrate into a quivering mass of organic matter. His body heat muddled her brain.

When the two of them came in contact it could only be described as chemistry, electrical conductivity, spontaneous combustion. Oh, how seriously pathetic to be reduced to bottom-level biological rubble by a man.

He slipped a key card into her palm, then pressed his lips to her ear and whispered in his robust Spanish accent, "Come to room 716 as soon as you can get away. I will be waiting."

THIRTY MINUTES LATER, a short, firm rap sounded at the door of room 716.

Forcing himself to remain calm and in control, he let her knock again before pulling open the door to find Catherine the Great leaning against the doorjamb looking like a billion bucks.

He was about to speak, to say something comforting to soothe their nervousness, when she took him totally and utterly by surprise. Meggie splayed a palm across his chest and pushed him back as she stepped over the threshold. With one delicately slippered foot, she slammed the door closed behind them at the same time as she wadded his shirt in her fist and pulled him forcefully toward her. Her green eyes lit up like a lynx's and she pounced on him, growling softly. His knees went weak with lust and he felt a curious tingling sensation in the back of his throat. She planted a kiss on him with such ravenous aggression that he found himself propelled backward onto the bed. She followed, melding her mouth to his, straddling his prone body and tugging his shirt from his waistband, all in one smooth move.

Her brazenness bowled him over. Holy buried treasure. What had he wrought?

He was both pleased and disconcerted by her overt onslaught. This wasn't the sensible, restrained Meggie Scofield he'd known his whole life. This was the lusty, uninhibited wench from his fantasies.

Wait a minute. Maybe he was dreaming all this. Maybe he should pinch himself.

But no, she was nibbling on his bottom lip with her straight white teeth, and it felt very real indeed. Apparently their role-playing had unleashed a long-dormant tempest within her.

She wrapped her arms around his neck, pressed her body against the length of him and eagerly ran her tongue over his lips.

No. Wait. Stop the presses. This wouldn't do. At the rate she was moving, he wouldn't last five minutes.

Reaching up, he untangled her hands from his hair

at the same time he disengaged his mouth from hers. He lifted her off him, placed her to one side and sat up.

"Sweetheart," Caleb crooned. "Slow down. This isn't a race."

She pulled back, her chest rising and falling rapidly. She blinked and then a red flush ran up her neck to color her cheeks.

"I'm sorry. I don't know what came over me. I've never acted like that."

He pulled her to him. "Shh...don't be embarrassed. I liked it. We just need to slow down."

"You're right." She nodded. "I guess I was just wanting to get to it before I lost my courage."

Aw hell.

Was she trying to rush through sex with him just to get it over with? Was she trying to prove something to herself, using him as a means to her end?

He took her hand. "I don't want you to do anything you don't want to do."

"I'm not," she insisted, and rested her head against his shoulder.

"Good." He exhaled, troubled by the unsettling sensation tromping around in his gut.

"But I do have two requests."

He would do absolutely anything for her, Caleb realized. If she asked him do handstands atop the Space Needle, he would have asked her how many and done one extra for good measure—even in the face of his fear of man-made heights. He would grant her every whim, from the simplest appeal to the most sublime demand. He wanted her that much.

"We must leave on our masks."

She didn't want to see his face. What did that mean? Caleb bit down on the inside of his cheek. He'd intended on revealing himself to her tonight, but he had promised to comply with her desires, and he was a man of his word.

"All right."

"And turn out the lights. All of them."

"Whatever you wish."

He did as she asked, drawing the curtains and turning off each lamp until the room was pitch-black, the way it had been that night in the cabin.

With no lights anywhere, he had to feel his way in the darkness. His other four senses pricked in awareness. He could not see her, but he felt her presence, heard her breathing, smelled the wonderful womanly scent of her, tasted her unique flavor on the tip of his tongue.

And he had to admit, not being able to see was highly erotic. The anticipation had been building for seven weeks and his nerves were taut as newly tuned guitar strings just waiting to be strummed.

He moved toward where she had been standing, but felt her slip past him.

She giggled. "Find me if you can."

Caleb smiled in the darkness. Obviously, she liked playing tag.

He lunged for her, came into contact with some soft part of her body, but she squirmed away before he could clamp a tight hold on her.

She pattered across the room, and he heard rustling noises.

Caleb went after her, his blood chugging through his veins, thick as syrup. He moved slowly, listening for sounds of her. He kept his arms outstretched, feeling for obstacles.

Table, chair, lamp.

"Where are you?"

Curtains. An armoire. The television set.

And then his hand brushed bare breasts, and the impact of connecting with her ripped through him like a detonated time bomb. He realized with a shock that Meggie had shed her clothing.

Like a blind man reading braille, he skimmed his palms over her smooth naked skin. He felt goose bumps raise on her flesh, and experienced a corresponding tactile reaction of his own.

She reached up to stroke her fingertips over his face and his body caught fire, singeing him internally from head to toe.

He cupped her pert full breasts in his hands and wished like the devil he could see the pink tips of her nipples poking out at him. He had to satisfy himself with tenderly pinching those straining buds until she murmured a soft, "Oh my."

He lowered his head, ran his tongue across first one nipple and then the other.

"You're wicked," she gasped.

"Isn't that why I intrigue you?"

"Yes, yes."

"You never know what I might do next."

She inhaled sharply.

"That's why you don't want me to remove my mask. You like an outlaw."

"Uh-huh."

He grasped her hands, raised them over her head and pinned her to the wall.

"You don't know what you're getting yourself into, *señorita.*" He had to force himself to stay in character as Don Juan although this game was driving him right over the edge of reason.

She was his prisoner now, trembling with excitement and need. "Please," she whimpered, "don't..."

"Don't what? Ravish you?" He'd sensed that she was taking their game to a new level, and he would play along.

He felt her nod, and a rush of blood drained straight to his groin.

"I could take you right here, right now. Up against the wall. Hard and fast. It's dark. You can't see my face. You couldn't even describe me to the authorities. It's best if you don't give me an excuse to punish you."

"But I've been a very bad girl. I've told the police where they can find you."

The playful tone in her voice let him know he hadn't gone too far. He amazed himself at the boundaries he was able to cross with her.

Helpless to resist her plea for more sex play, and wanting to give her as much pleasure as he possibly could before taking his own release, Caleb lowered her arms to her sides and then sank to his knees.

"Uh-oh. That means I'm going to have to give you a thorough tongue-lashing."

He spanned the curve of her waist with his hands and then slowly began to run his tongue from her rib cage to her navel. She entangled her fingers in his hair and clasped him tightly against her belly. His mask must have scratched her tender flesh for she made a moaning, mewling sound of heightened awareness that nourished his own arousal. He ran a hand down the voluptuous curve of her hip to cup her buttocks, and discovered she still wore thong panties and thigh-high stockings.

Man alive. She was volcano hot and seducing him without even moving.

He hooked his thumbs under the ribbon of silk hugging those spectacularly feminine hips and started the exhilarating procedure of inching the flimsy morsel of fabric down her warm, firm thighs. She gasped, an erotic sound that reverberated like a prayer in his head.

When he feathered his fingertips along her skin in languid exploration, her grip on his hair tightened. He touched the inside of her thigh, the top of her legs, drew circles on her tight fanny. He stroked every inch of the area between her navel and knees, except where he knew she most wanted him to touch.

"You're vicious," she moaned. "I thought you promised me a tongue-lashing."

"Punishment, sweetheart, takes many forms."

"Bastard!" She uttered the word with clenched teeth.

He laughed.

She leaned back against the wall and arched her pelvis up toward him, planting her womanhood right near his face. Begging.

"Brazen wench," he declared.

"If you can't take the heat, then get out of the kitchen."

"I'll ignore that, because I know you don't really mean it."

Her sigh in response was like a caress in the darkness, inching down his spine, spilling through his bloodstream, setting him on fire with escalating desire for her. Swelling need seized him and his pulse knocked wildly in his temple. To wrest back a modicum of restrait, he compelled himself to disregard the provocative smell of her, the seductive rhythm of her undulating hips, by resolutely turning his attention back to the thong caught around her knees.

He skimmed the scrap of satin down to her ankles, his hands brushing against the enticing silkiness of her nylons.

"Step out of your panties," he demanded.

She obeyed.

"You really are as mercurial as the wind," he said. "One minute aggressive, the next coy, the next acquiescent. Who are you, really?"

"My identity is secret, just as you are a complete mystery to me."

She liked not knowing him. Controlled, sensible, honest-to-a-fault Meggie liked adventure and rowdiness and subterfuge in the bedroom. As long as he remained behind the mask, as long as he was the sensual, roguish Don Juan, he could provide her with all the things she needed. But what could he do for her as plain, ordinary Caleb Greenleaf? The unsettling thought disturbed him and quashed his libido.

But not for long.

"I'm naked, and now you must get naked, too," she declared.

The mental imagine of her standing completely unclothed before him dispelled his self-doubts and goaded illicit visions of untying his leather pants, freeing his ferocious erection and plummeting deep inside her feminine recess.

But not yet. She deserved much more than a blazing quickie.

She began unbuttoning his shirt, her cool fingers tracking lightly over the heated flesh she slowly unveiled. She plunged her fingers into the curls of hair on his chest.

Caleb groaned, clasped her to him and delivered a series of searingly desperate kisses to her smooth, flat belly. She moaned and slid her body down his until she was on her knees in front of him, her breath flowing hot and fast against his skin.

She explored him with her honeyed tongue, tasting the skin she uncovered while completing the task of removing his shirt. She stripped it off his shoulders and over his biceps before flinging the garment across the room. Splaying her palms against his chest, Meggie muttered a pleased sound of discovery and traced her fingers down his torso to the hard planes of his stomach. His body tensed and flexed in response to her inquisitive, reverential exploration.

"I wish I could see you," he croaked.

"No," she said sharply. "No lights."

He wanted to ask why, but dammit if she didn't start licking his ear in the provocative way she'd done in the ballroom. The very same maneuver that had caused him to press the room card key in her hand and invite her up for a midnight romp. It seemed they both operated better in disguise.

Was secrecy what fed the flame between them? What would happen once the mystery was gone?

Caleb didn't want to think about that eventuality.

He didn't want to think about anything. He just wanted to be in the moment.

As a man accustomed to spending much time alone in the wilderness, appreciating and living in the moment was his specialty. He could give both Meggie and himself the gift of total concentration. He would. Just for tonight, no more doubts, no more fears of what might happen once she discovered a familiar face behind the Don Juan mask.

"Nibble on my neck," Meggie requested in a jagged whisper.

His blood pulsed, fiery and brutal. As if hypnotized, he followed her instruction. Nestling his mouth to the hollow of her slender throat, he bared his teeth against her fevered skin. She cried out and squirmed against him when he took her flesh into his mouth and nipped lightly. He shivered in awe that he'd produced this reaction in her.

The taste of her succulent saltiness wasn't nearly enough. He was famished for her. Had been for years. He nibbled on her like a banquet feast, sucking and licking, swirling his tongue over the sweetness of her. Caleb plunged his fingers through her hair and cradled her naked body in his arms.

She was all soft swells and generous curves. Her nipples thrust hard against his chest, begging for attention. He left her neck and went straight for the eager buds, curling his tongue around one puckered peak and gently tugging. She hissed like a hot griddle doused with ice-cold water.

"You inflame me."

"Shh. Don't talk, just lick."

He laved her with his mouth. A tremble shuddered

through her and a slow, deep groan unfurled from her throat.

"That's it, don't stop."

He savored her, claimed her and ached to possess her on a baser level. He gorged on the sugary taste of her, indulging his whims.

Caleb caressed her with his hands, kneaded her skin, massaged her, quickly learning which spots produced the most explosive reactions. He discovered where she liked it firm and where she preferred a whisper-light touch. Which stroke made her quiver and which made her sigh with restless longing.

Steadily, relentlessly, he pushed her toward the edge of reason. He experienced it, too—the heady anticipation, the measured buildup, the escalating wildness.

She strained her hips against the hard ridge of his erection. He knew what she wanted because he wanted the same thing. Wanted it more than he had ever wanted anything in his life. Passion throbbed between them, blistering them both. They hovered on the verge of stepping completely out of bounds of all rational behavior.

Whimpering, she sought his mouth and kissed him with a yearning, soulful need.

Scuttling his hands up her naked back, he crushed her to him, hugging her breasts—still damp from his tongue—tightly against his chest. Their hearts raced in unison, ratcheting upward in a building crescendo. Frenziedly, he dragged his mouth from hers, gasping for air and attempting to stay his frantic lust.

God, how he wanted to see her face, to examine

her eyes and learn exactly what she was feeling. Did she want him as much as he wanted her?

Stupid question.

Even as he sought a small respite from this ever-increasing whirlwind of want, Meggie clearly had another plan in mind. To garner his notice, she bit down lightly on his earlobe and tugged the susceptible flesh with her teeth.

"Show me what you like, Don Juan. Take my hand. Guide me where you want me to go."

"Ah, *señorita,* it is my place to please you, not the other way around," he managed to gasp. If she were to suddenly start plying those lips of hers in his most sensitive areas, he wouldn't last two seconds.

"This can't be one-sided like that night in the cabin. I have to know I can please you as much as you please me."

He shook his head.

"You must. It's very important to me."

"All right," he said with an exasperated groan. "If it really means that much to you."

Spellbound, he plunged his fingers through the silky strands of her hair and began with a long, heartfelt kiss simply because he could not get enough of the flavor and texture of her mouth. He leaned backward, taking her with him until he was splayed flat on his back and she was straddling him.

After a few heated minutes, he tenderly broke off the connection and gently steered her moist, parted lips down his chin, over his throat and, in measured increments, along his chest.

Her tongue fluttered across his ridged nipples, and she did to him what he'd earlier done to her. She was making every single one of his most forbidden fantasies come true, and he loved her for it.

She tracked a path from his nipples to his belly, scooting her bare fanny down his leather-clad thighs as she moved lower, ever lower.

Although he wished he could see her, there was something unspeakably erotic about total darkness—not being able to spot her next move, unable to predict what else she had up her sleeve, because he wasn't privy to the naughty gleam in her eyes.

Everywhere her mouth touched, his skin sizzled. He moaned as her lips traveled to where his belly hair disappeared into his waistband. When she stretched her mouth over his hardness through the pliant leather of his pants, he almost came right then and there.

He raised his hips and hissed with sharp, greedy need. "That's it."

She drew back and her fingers went to work on the drawstrings at his fly. Without faltering, she tugged his pants past his hips and chortled out loud when she realized he wasn't wearing underwear.

"You're going commando." She giggled, obviously delighted by the fact.

"No boxers or briefs for Don Juan."

"Guess with those drawstrings you don't have to worry about anything...er...important getting caught in a zipper."

Her lighthearted, teasing tone touched his heart. She was happy. He'd made her happy.

She wrapped a hand around his rock-hard penis and his smile vanished as he fought his natural instinct to explode at her searing touch.

"And my, Don Juan, may I say, what an impressive package you have."

"The better to—" He almost said "make love to you with, Little Red Riding Hood," but he figured "make love" was the last thing she wanted to hear. Instead he used a crude street term that seemed to rev her engines, for she made short work of his pants, peeling them right off his body.

"That's right, talk dirty to me."

She returned her attention to his throbbing organ, and he was unable to speak at all, much less talk dirty. She stroked him with her fingers, squeezing and rubbing, revelling in the raw and ready hotness of his sex, exploring the paradoxical velvet and granite texture.

Tentatively, she sheathed her mouth around him, tasting his masculine essence with the tip of her tongue. She ran her lips up and down his shaft in a maneuver that caused his entire body to quake helplessly.

Oh mercy. Mercy.

She took her time, trying out a variety of experiments. She blew hot little puffs of air against his skin. She swirled her tongue around the head of his penis. She sucked and licked, teasing him, drawing him ever closer to the brink of climax.

He shuddered when she discovered the sensitive ridge lurking below the proud, jutting tip. In that moment, he almost called out her name. In fact, the first syllable was past his lips when he remembered the game and her rules. He bit down on his tongue.

"Mmm."

"You like?"

"If you keep doing what you're doing, then we're both in trouble."

"Good."

Before Caleb knew what was happening, she took his engorged shaft as deeply into her mouth as she could possibly manage in a blinding, white-hot kiss that turned his world inside out. He whimpered as she engulfed him in a way that made him absolutely mad-dog crazy for release. For her.

His hands searched for her in the darkness, clutched her hair in desperation and tried to get her to break contact. If she didn't quit he simply would not be able to stop the force of nature that had kidnapped his body.

But she would not be denied.

He gasped, he writhed.

She moved faster, sucked harder.

He could not think. Could not reason. Could only let himself be swept up in her vortex.

Up, up, up, she took him. Climbing higher and higher. When she gently cupped his balls in the palm of one hand, he knew it was the end for him. Every muscle in his body tensed. He stopped breathing and for one brief second in time felt as if he hung suspended on the edge of the world.

The searing orgasm red-hot and mind-blowingly powerful, shot up through his shaft in a blinding rush. Intense, blistering pleasure shuddered throughout his system in a kaleidoscope of sensation.

He tried to pull her away but she ignored his attempts. The moist, warm recesses of her mouth stole his restraint, and he could do absolutely nothing but ride the roller coaster down, down, down as he plummeted earthward into heavenly release.

Meggie! Meggie!

What a gift. What a surprise. What a woman.

Emotion pressed into the corners of his eyes, and for the first time since turning out the lights, he was grateful she couldn't see him.

Panting, she raised her head and whispered in his ear. "Make love to me with your mouth, Don Juan. Make love to me right now."

8

TAKE A RISK, she had told herself when she'd accepted Don Juan's key card. *Take a chance. No telling what you might discover about yourself.*

Boy, had that been an understatement.

She knelt beside Don Juan, trembling in the darkness, stunned and amazed at what she had just done. She'd never done anything so intimate with a man before.

How would he react? What would he do?

In answer to her question, he gave a groan and she felt him get to his feet. He fumbled for her in the darkness and latched his arms around her waist with a possessiveness that both frightened Meggie and delighted her. Without speaking, he scooped her into his arms and gingerly made his way to the bed.

What was it about him that drew her? What made her yearn to throw caution aside and proceed with the reckless abandon of a horny teenager? He fascinated her like no one else on earth, and she didn't even know his real name.

This is just for tonight, Meggie. Don't for a moment forget that. You can lose your head if you wish, but don't give this guy your heart.

But of course not. She had learned her lesson the hard way. Don Juan was a dalliance to help her repair her shattered self-esteem. As long as she understood that, she wouldn't get hurt.

By providing her with a safe outlet for sexual exploration, Don Juan was giving Meggie her femininity back. Because of his precious gift, when she did find the right man and fall in love, she would come to her new lover with a free heart. Whatever happened tonight, the knowledge that she would be better prepared for a loving relationship in the future because of Don Juan buoyed her hopes.

She could find love again. She would. And next time, it would be with the right guy.

Tonight, however, was about cutting loose, experimenting and finding out just how far her limits stretched.

Don Juan deposited her gently in the middle of the mattress. He stepped back and she reached for him.

Sudden fear struck her. What if he wasn't taking this affair as casually as she? She didn't want to hurt him any more than she wanted to be hurt.

"Don Juan?"

"Yes?" His sexy, disembodied voice floated from the blackness, causing her to shiver with expectation.

God, how she loved the way he spoke. Never mind that the accent was fake. She knew he wasn't really Spanish, but she ignored that knowledge for the sake of fantasy, and reminded herself she would not ruin everything by delving into reality.

"This is just a game for you, isn't it? I'm just one in a long string of your lovers. Right?"

He said nothing. Silence roared in her ears. Oh, no. What if he wanted more than she could give? She wasn't about to get involved with another rogue, no matter how sexy or how good at foreplay he might be.

"Right?"

"Remember," he whispered at last. "I'm here for one thing and one thing only. Your pleasure. Do you understand?"

Relief washed through her. Yes. The last thing she wanted was to hurt him. Thank heavens they were on the same wavelength, because it would have been next to impossible to walk away from him at this point.

She felt the mattress sag from his weight as he settled himself on the bed. From nowhere, it seemed, his fingers made contact with her arm and roved up her shoulder to her collarbone and then down to her aching, engorged breasts.

"I want to reward you. To thank you for the perfect present you just gave me. I wish to reciprocate."

Meggie hitched in a deep breath as his fingers trailed lower, inch by exquisite inch.

"You are so beautiful."

"I'm not beautiful." She laughed. "You've only seen me in a mask, with a costume on. For all you know I look like Quasimodo."

"And I could say the same. Isn't that part of the attraction? Not knowing what is behind the mask and getting excited anyway?"

"Yes," she admitted, and moistened her lips with her tongue.

His fingers were getting closer, ever closer, to the place where she wanted him to be.

"I could be anyone. No?"

"Yes."

"That excites you, doesn't it?"

"Uh-huh."

He stroked her lower abdomen, stoking the flames that were building inside her. After several minutes of this, her entire body was rigid and she wanted to grab him by the hair and tell him to get on with it.

When she didn't think she could stand the teasing one second longer, he let his hand drift to the hair at the juncture between her legs. Gently he stroked a finger over her right upper thigh.

"Open for me. Nothing is more erotic then the moment a woman parts her legs for her lover."

He didn't have to ask twice. Meggie shifted, moved her legs apart, welcomed him in, opened herself to the greatest vulnerability a woman could experience.

"The holiest of holy spots. The gate to heaven."

He made her feel attractive and powerful and womanly. His reverential sigh brought a tightness to her chest. No wonder women fell at Don Juan's feet. He was irresistible.

And then his hot, wet mouth was on her. He kissed her belly, while his cheek caressed her soft, bushy thatch of hair.

She realized then he wasn't wearing his mask, and panic gripped her. What if she saw his face?

Calm down, calm down.

The room was dark. She would insist he put his mask back on before turning on the lights. Besides, she couldn't freak out right now because the things he was doing to her down there were way beyond her realm of experience.

"Sweetheart," Don Juan murmured. "I want to drink you up."

"Yes. Yes, please."

He was between her parted thighs, his head lowered. She tensed, waiting.

And then he slipped his tongue inside her dewy folded flesh and licked her. One small quick flick, as if getting a drop of ice cream before it melted off the cone and ran down his hand.

She gasped.

"Mmm, you taste delicious."

A sigh escaped her.

"You are so hot, so wet."

"You make me that way."

She felt his lips, which were pressed against her, curl up in a grin. Oh, he was arrogant about his prowess, but with good reason.

He unwrapped her like savoring the opening of a birthday present, using his tongue to explore layer after layer. The ridges and folds of her womanhood blossomed beneath his seductive ministrations. She felt the delicate tissue swell in sultry response to his devilish sucking as his saliva mixed with her natural juices.

He changed tempo. Whereas before he'd been delivering light, rapid flicks over her protruding cleft, he dawdled and pressed more firmly.

Slow, long, deep strokes. Down, then up, in a mesmerizing configuration.

"Aaah."

"So you like things nice and slow."

She nodded her head and twisted her fingers through his hair. "Stop talking."

He laughed and returned to his task. He varied his patterns. One minute circles, the next a grid, after that a haphazard zigzag. Meggie felt a gigantic pressure building beneath the hood of her cleft, building and growing and throbbing.

Ever so slightly he nibbled on her inner lips, and she just about leaped off the bed, the sensation was so excruciatingly incredible.

"More. More." She trembled and clutched the bedspread in her fists.

Sucking very gently, he drew her cleft into his mouth. In and out. In and out. Tugging. Releasing. Tugging. Releasing.

Entranced by the erotic decadence of the act, Meggie could do nothing but enjoy. How was it she didn't feel tense and anxious about this? What was different about Don Juan?

Because he's a stranger.

Odd that she could let down her guard with a man she didn't know, and allow him do the most private things to her when she'd had trouble relaxing and letting go in the midst of a long-term relationship.

You weren't in the right relationship.

She'd been with Jesse for all the wrong reasons, and she knew it. Jesse had been her ticket out of Alaska, and she'd lived vicariously through his wild ways. But now, no matter how irrational her actions might seem to her practical self, she was having her own adventure, embracing life on her own terms.

It felt damn good. No more taking care of other people's needs first. This time, she was doing what was right for Meggie.

Don Juan glided his silken tongue around the tiny base of her, and then skated up to the tender, surging tip. The hood of her cleft slid back and the sensitive nubbin strained for his attention.

There was danger here. One slip of his teeth and the fun would be all over.

But he understood. He was a careful lover. Oh, so very careful. Everything he did elicited unbelievable tides of carnal bliss.

She shivered and quivered and groaned.

He blew a steady stream of cool air against her, before returning to the hot licking. He alternated: chilly air; scalding, wet tongue. Frosty, fiery, icy, boiling, until Meggie thought she wouldn't be able to bear this sweet torment one second longer.

But he wasn't finished.

On and on he went until she lay limp, wrung out, and when he gently inserted one finger inside her, she lost all self-respect.

"Make me come," she cried out. "Please. Make me come. Now!"

The ache that had been coiling tighter and tighter inside her unfurled then in one blinding, clear starburst that radiated outward in an exploding rush.

No one had ever brought her to orgasm this way. Tears sprang to her eyes, and as she shuddered and trembled, Don Juan positioned himself beside her on the bed and drew her into his arms.

He kissed her tenderly, hauntingly. He tasted of her feminine flavor. Full and rich, robust and healthy. Nothing had ever tasted so sexy. Meggie snuggled into his body, rested her head against his chest and, in her warm, sated state, happily fell asleep.

NEVER IN HIS LIFE had Caleb known such total rapture. And to think he had been so very afraid that making love with Meggie could never live up to his teenage fantasies. Instead, their glorious encounter had exceeded all his previous expectations.

The woman was better than his most provocative daydream. One more night with her was not going to be nearly enough. That much was clear.

He lay in the darkness listening to her breathing. She was spooned into him, her fanny curled against him, his arm thrown over her waist. He squeezed her tighter and his gut clenched.

He wanted more of this.

Of her.

But first, he had to come clean and tell her the truth—that he, Caleb Greenleaf, was her secret Don Juan lover. What was the best way to do that? Let her wake up, look over and see his face?

Nah. He immediately discarded the idea. Too jarring. He didn't want her to regret their night together, and if he didn't handle this just right he ran the risk of having her never speak to him again. He had to find another way, a better time and place to reveal himself to her.

But where and how?

He would have to think about it. In the meantime, he was going to have to slip from the room while she slept.

Inwardly, he groaned. The last thing he wanted to do was leave this bed and her warm, soft body. He wanted to languish here, savor this moment. He wanted to wake her with kisses and make love to her all over again, not just with his mouth this time. He wanted to be inside her, consume her, claim her as his own.

But he wouldn't. He couldn't. She wasn't ready to learn the truth. If she had been, she wouldn't have insisted he douse the lights.

Caleb wondered if deep down inside somewhere she knew that he was Don Juan and she simply couldn't face the reality. That thought caused a twinge of anxiety to pierce his heart. His fingers gently stroked her sleeping form, and sorrow paralleled desire in the immense complexity of these new emotions.

He wasn't going to pursue that line of thought. For now, he would do what he had to do, even though the thought of leaving her was killing him.

Much as it hurt, he had to go.

MEGGIE AWOKE WITH A START, confused and disoriented. The hotel room was still dark, but sunlight shadows were seeping beneath the drawn curtains, casting enough illumination to let her see that the space on the bed beside her was empty.

Breathing in a deep sigh, she pushed her tangled hair from her face and sat up.

"Don Juan?" she called, thinking he might be in the bathroom. If he was in there and not wearing his mask, she didn't want to see him.

The thought of coming face-to-face with her lover caused her pulse to accelerate. She threw back the covers and hopped out of bed. But she needn't have worried. He didn't answer, and no sounds came from behind the closed bathroom door.

She knocked. No response.

Whew. That was a relief!

Okay, so if she was so happy that he'd abandoned her, why the heavy sadness settling low in her belly? Was this the morning-after-a-one-night-stand blues? She stepped into the bathroom and flicked on the light.

"Eeek!"

Who was that woman in the mirror? Her lips were slightly swollen, her hair a rat's nest, her mascara-smeared eyes like a raccoon.

She studied herself for a long moment. The thought of Don Juan hung like a mist between herself and her reflection. As if in a dream, she saw him before her. She gazed at that shadowy image, memorizing it to forever carry him with her, knowing she would treasure it for fear if it might break up and scatter like paperweight snowflakes.

"Stop being so fanciful," she told her reflection. "It's not like you."

She had no reason to feel blue or abandoned. She had nothing to complain about. She'd gotten what she wanted—a thrilling night of no-strings-attached sex. Raw, animal intimacy to help her overcome her fears and regain her femininity.

"Don't feel sad, Meggie. You just reclaimed your sexuality," she declared to her bedraggled reflection in the mirror. "Be happy. Be proud. Go forth from this moment knowing that you are not dull and predictable either in bed or out."

She made herself grin.

Feeling a little better, she showered and dressed, then realized she was going to have to sneak out of the hotel room just after dawn, wearing her Catherine the Great costume and no makeup. Hopefully she wouldn't run into anybody she knew.

"Better get a move on, Scofield," she muttered under her breath.

Groaning, she slipped her feet into her high-heeled shoes and headed for the door. That's when she saw it dangling from the doorknob.

Don Juan's mask.

That was all? No note requesting to see her again? No phone number where she could reach him?

But that was a good thing. Right?

Except she did want to see him again. No matter how irrational the thought.

If you want to know who he is, it's easy to find out. All you have to do is call the front desk and ask who reserved this room.

Quickly, she slammed the door on that idea. She did not wish to pursue a long-term relationship with the man. It was over.

For the longest moment she stared at the mask, trying to find a double meaning that wasn't there. This was it then. With a sigh—of disappointment or relief, she couldn't say which—Meggie balled the mask in her fist and flung it into the wastepaper basket.

9

''WHERE HAVE YOU BEEN?'' Wendy demanded, sizing up Meggie's bedraggled costume. She was sitting on Meggie's front stoop, the Sunday morning newspaper tucked under one arm, a box of doughnuts resting on her bent knees. ''I've been ringing your doorbell for a good ten minutes.''

''You got Krispy Kremes? I love you.''

Meggie reached for the doughnuts in an attempt to sidetrack her friend, but Wendy was having none of it. She hunched forward, shielding the box with her body.

''No way, sister. You don't get one until you tell me where you were.''

''You're not my mother,'' Meggie said defensively. She didn't want to talk about her night with Don Juan. It was too special.

Besides, she was afraid that if she spoke of their lovemaking, and of how he had left her without a single word, she would start crying. For no good reason at all. She had *wanted* a no-strings-attached fling. What was there to bawl about?

''No talkie, no Krispy Kreme.''

''Fine. Keep your doughnuts.'' She stepped around Wendy to insert her key in her door lock.

Looking startled, Wendy jumped to her feet and

followed Meggie into her apartment. ''You're seriously turning down doughnuts?''

''Seriously.'' She tossed her keys on the table and kicked off her shoes.

''Ooh, this must be really juicy.'' Wendy opened up the doughnut box and fanned the lid. ''Mmm, smell. Got your favorite. Plain glazed.''

''Forget it. I'm not talking.''

''If it was the other way around, I would tell you.'' Wendy pursed her lips in a pout.

''That's beside the point. You love to blab.'' Meggie pulled a carton of orange juice from the refrigerator. ''Want some?''

''With doughnuts? Yeck. You've gotta be kiddin'.''

''Suit yourself.'' She shrugged and poured a glass for herself.

Wendy set the doughnuts on the counter. ''I'm getting kinda worried about you, Megs.''

''Don't be.''

''How can I not? You're my best friend. And at first, when you came back from Alaska all charged up after your romantic encounter with this Don Juan dude, I thought it was really cool the way you were taking charge of your life. Cutting your hair, getting new clothes and speaking up for yourself at work.''

''But now?''

''Well.'' Wendy eyed Meggie's rumpled dress. ''You're not acting like the Meggie I know and love. I mean, obviously you were with some man last night.''

Meggie said nothing.

''Why won't you tell me?''

"It's personal."

Wendy slapped her palm over her mouth. "Omigosh. It's that hometown guy. You spent the night with your old buddy."

"Caleb? Don't be silly. His plane isn't even due in until this afternoon. Of course I wasn't with Caleb. Why would you think I was with Caleb? I told you I don't have romantic feelings for Caleb."

Meggie realized she was talking too fast, denying Wendy's accusations too vehemently and using Caleb's name too often. Why?

And why the sudden tightness in her breasts at the thought of making love with Caleb? Good grief! What a mental picture. Maybe she was losing all control when it came to men. Maybe Don Juan had turned her into a sex-crazed nympho.

"I don't know. Whenever you talk about Caleb, your eyes light up and you get this glow about you."

"You're nuts."

"Then who *were* you with?"

"I don't want to discuss it."

"Oh no." Wendy groaned. "It's that Don Juan dude, isn't it?"

Meggie looked away, refusing to meet her gaze.

Wendy bit her bottom lip. "I care about you and I'm afraid you're getting in over your head. You know after going through a divorce some women go wild and do things they would normally never do. Things they regret afterward. Don't get swept away by lust, Meggie."

"I appreciate your concern, I really do. But I really am okay."

"Promise?"

Meggie nodded.

"All right then, but if you need anything, anything at all, I'm here."

"Thank you for that. Now, if you don't mind, I think I'd like to take a nap."

Wendy nodded. "I'll leave you a couple of Krispy Kremes, even if you won't tell me about your sordid night of pleasure."

"It wasn't sordid."

"What fun is that?" Wendy grinned impishly.

"Go on, get out of here."

"See you later." Wendy put three doughnuts on a saucer, covered them with a paper towel and then retreated with the box.

After Meggie closed the door behind her friend, she wandered into the living room, intent on checking her answering machine. The green light blinked. One message.

A bubble of hope expanded inside her. Maybe Don Juan had called to tell her what a wonderful time he'd had. Or maybe he'd even called to make another date for the next time he was in town.

Don't be ridiculous. You made it clear you didn't want to see him again. He didn't call.

She depressed the play button, crossed her fingers and strained to hear the voice spilling into the room.

"Hi."

For one moment she thought it *was* Don Juan.

"Meggie, this is Caleb."

She exhaled and sank onto the sofa. Why was she so disappointed?

"I just called to let you know I got into Seattle a little early, so you don't have to pick me up at the airport. I'm staying at the Crowne Plaza. I've got some things to do today, so I guess I'll catch you at the lecture tomorrow. Can't wait to see you. Bye."

Well, at least somebody wanted to see her. So what if she never heard from Don Juan again? No sense feeling sorry for herself. It was all for the best. Besides, Caleb was in town. If anyone could cheer her up, that man, with his understanding smile and soulful blue eyes, most certainly could.

DESPITE THE LOSS of his notes and reference material, the lecture was going really well. Caleb knew his entomology as intimately as he now knew Meggie's luscious body.

He fielded questions and comments from the audience, which consisted of various medical personnel interested in knowing what they could do to educate the public about Lyme disease and related illnesses. He hadn't made a single mistake.

That is, until Meggie slipped in through a side door and took a seat on the aisle just a few feet from the podium.

He had been in the middle of a sentence, but the moment he spotted her, every bit of knowledge he possessed flew from his head. She looked exquisitely gorgeous, no matter that she wore shapeless pink hospital scrubs and not a speck of makeup. A catwalk supermodel would not have looked any better to him.

"The...er, I...um," he said, desperately wishing he had papers to shuffle, a pencil to tap, anything to help him focus.

Meggie caught his eye, broke into a beaming smile

that lit her face from corner to corner and winked at him.

"Sorry I'm late," she mouthed silently.

His heart pinched. A half-dozen conflicting emotions converged upon him, clogging his throat and tightening his chest. Guilt, excitement, longing, fear, desire and inexplicable tenderness.

Thoughts of Saturday night flooded his mind. He recalled those lips, soft as rose petals and tasty as taffy. How he wished he could have kissed her awake Sunday morning, massaged her taxed muscles and then served her breakfast in bed.

Instead, because of this deception he had been forced to perpetuate, he had slipped from her bed, sheepish and embarrassed. He wondered what she'd thought when she found the mask dangling from the doorknob, and if he'd hurt her feelings by leaving her without so much as a goodbye kiss.

Had she awakened in the cold dark and reached for him, only to find him missing? Had she looked for comfort and found only sharp emptiness?

Perhaps he was being fanciful. Perhaps she was relieved he'd crept away like a sneaky thief, glad she did not have to face him in the sobering light of day and discover his true identity.

He looked at her and his heart tore.

She was still smiling. She wriggled her fingers. She seemed fine. In fact, there was a distinct sparkle in her eyes he hadn't seen there in a very long time.

Apparently orgasms with unknown masked men agreed with her.

Jealousy clenched his jaw.

Dumb-ass, you were that masked man. What? Are you envious of yourself?

Yeah, okay. Maybe he was the guy who'd put the rosy color in her cheeks, but it just as easily could have been someone else.

Caleb realized he was staring at her and silence had settled over the room, while everyone waited for him to speak. But he couldn't continue. He had no idea what to say next.

"Why don't we take a break for lunch?" He glanced at his watch. "The lecture will resume in one hour."

He had to talk to her and find out how she was doing. He had to make sure he hadn't irreparably harmed her.

She rose to her feet. He stepped off the podium and hurried toward her.

Calm down. Chill out. Take it easy.

"Meggie," he said, feeling rather awkward and unsure of himself.

What now?

"Caleb." Her smile crinkled the corners of her green eyes in a way that rendered him useless. She held out her arms and motioned him closer. "Come here and give me a hug. It's so darn good to see you."

And so he embraced her, pressing her tightly against him and patting her back. She smelled fragrantly sweet, like springtime in the Tongass. They were friends, after all. The hug meant nothing more to her than *good to see you, old buddy* and he knew it.

But that didn't stop him from wishing and praying for more. Her body heat infiltrated his consciousness on a primordial level and sent a bolt of desire shooting through his groin.

This wouldn't do. He had to get away from her before he got hard and she discovered that her good old buddy wanted to be *way* more than just friends.

He stepped from the circle of her embrace and looked into her eyes. She gazed at him, a quizzical expression on her face. She blinked and the look was gone. Had she begun to suspect he was Don Juan?

In that moment, he almost confessed everything, but something about the way she was looking at him now, as if she were honestly happy and excited about him being in Seattle, rendered him mute.

This clearly wasn't the time or place for true confessions.

"I'm taking you to lunch," she declared. "There's a lovely little French bistro on the corner."

He nodded, tongue-tied.

She squeezed his hand. "You'll never know how pleased I am that you decided to teach the symposiums. For one thing, we were in desperate need of a knowledgeable instructor, but the truth is I've really missed you since I left Alaska."

"You're kidding. You missed me?"

"Of course I'm not kidding, doofus." She slung her arm over his shoulder, leaned into him and reached up a hand to tousle his hair. "You're my surrogate kid brother."

His hopes sputtered and died.

Surrogate kid brother. Not exactly the sentiment he was hoping for. When he finally got around to telling her that he was Don Juan, he would remind her exactly why he'd been forced into this pretense.

She refused to see him for the grown man he was and not the gangly teen he'd once been. The Don Juan outfit had been the only way to burrow under her prejudices and expand her mind.

Problem was, would she appreciate the underhanded education?

MEGGIE PEERED AT CALEB over the rim of her teacup. It was a little after one o'clock and they were sitting across from each at other at La Maison sharing a thick turkey croissant and bowls of hearty French onion soup.

Damn, but she'd never really noticed how very handsome he was. There was no way she was going to get out of introducing him to Wendy. If she refused, her friend might never speak to her again. Good-looking, caring men like Caleb didn't come along every day. He would be good for Wendy, who had a tendency to get tangled up with freeloaders.

But would Wendy be good for Caleb?

Why do you care so much? Introduce them and they can sort it out for themselves.

She had enough problems of her own without fretting over other people's love lives. Absently, she fingered her lips, her thoughts traveling back to Don Juan and the erotic night she'd spent in his arms.

Truthfully, she was still a little shaky over what had transpired, both shocked and pleased by her uncharacteristic behavior.

Does it stick out all over me? Have I changed? Am I different? Can people tell by looking at me? Can Caleb?

She shot another glance his way and found him

studying her with such a peculiar expression on his face that for one halting moment she believed he must be privy to her every thought and know exactly what she'd been up to.

But that was fanciful nonsense. How on earth could Caleb possibly know that she'd been with Don Juan?

And if he did know, why would he even care?

Embarrassment frosted over her like an icy film, followed by an unexpected blast of heat. She felt her face flush pink.

This had to stop. Her obsessing over Don Juan was beginning to bleed over into other aspects of her life, causing her to imagine all kinds of crazy things.

Not good. Not good at all.

Meggie peeped up at Caleb again. He was still staring at her as if she were some ageless riddle he couldn't quite decipher.

"Umm, delicious soup," she said, although the soup could have been swamp water for all the flavor her taste buds registered.

"Excellent choice of restaurants."

His comment sounded forced, or was she imagining things? Surely Caleb was no different than usual. He'd always been quiet, observant, contemplative. His steady, unwavering calmness was what she liked most about him.

Maybe guilt was causing her to read more into his expression than was there. She cringed, imagining what he would say if he knew she'd just had a two-night-stand with Don Juan. He would probably be as protective as her brother Quinn and want to beat the guy up.

Ack!

This was one of the reasons she no longer lived in Bear Creek. Too many people knew her too well and tried to run interference for her when life didn't go her way.

But what was she saying? Life simply couldn't be better. Thanks to Don Juan, she'd found herself again. She had nothing to be ashamed of and everything to be grateful for.

"Penny for your thoughts," Caleb said.

"What?" She blinked.

The corner of his full mouth tipped up in a rueful grin. "You've been a thousand miles away. Is it the company?"

"Oh, no. I'm sorry."

"Trouble at work?"

She shook her head.

"Come on, you can talk to me. This is your buddy Caleb."

"It's nothing. Honest. I was just woolgathering."

"Okay. But if you ever need to talk..." He patted his shoulders. "These are pretty broad."

"Thanks." She smiled.

He was just the nicest guy. She was most definitely going to have to introduce him to Wendy. They both deserved someone special.

And right now Caleb deserved her undivided attention. Resolutely, she relegated all thoughts of Don Juan to a closet in her mind, stuffing him in there as her first skeleton.

She folded her hands one on top of the other. "So, tell me, how's the wife search going?"

He shrugged. "I've given up on that."

"Really? How come? That ad in *Metropolitan* worked wonders for Quinn and Mack and Jake."

"Yeah, but you know me, Meggie. I need my space, and here were all these strange women crowding me. I couldn't help but wonder if they wanted to be with me or with my money."

"Oh. I keep forgetting you're rich."

"Well, you're the only one."

"Not all women are gold diggers."

"Like my mother, you mean?"

"I didn't say that."

"No. You're too nice to criticize. But I haven't given up on the idea of getting married. I've just decided to let nature take its course. I'm not answering any more correspondence from the ad, and to tell you the truth, that's why I accepted the lecturer position. I needed to get out of town."

"Bear Creek can be kind of claustrophobic," Meggie admitted with a laugh, "despite the wide expanse of geography."

"Tell me about it."

Caleb tilted his head and looked at her in the light through the stained-glass window. Her silky hair glistened darkly; her green eyes sparkled, verdant and alive. She was so pretty and seemed to have no idea how appealing she looked bare faced and smiling. No artifice, no disguises.

Son of a bear, if he didn't ache to claim her right then and there, consequences be damned. He wanted to drive his fists into his thighs and bellow her name with such passion that every diner in the place would turn to stare at him. He wanted to wrap his hand around the nape of her neck and pull her across the table in a kiss so fierce it left no doubt what he needed from her. He wanted to jump to his feet, scoop her into his arms and carry her all the way back to Bear Creek like a caveman, a Viking, a marauding pirate.

Instead, he did the polite, civilized thing and lied through his teeth.

"You've got a little something there on the side of your mouth." He pointed with his index finger.

"Oh?" She raised a hand to the right side of her mouth and brushed at the nonexistent particle.

"The other side."

She dabbed a finger at the left side of her mouth. "Did I get it?"

"Allow me." Caleb leaned across the table and gently swept his thumb along her lower lip.

The contact was electric.

Meggie's eyes widened.

His heart thumped.

"Did you get it?" she whispered.

"Uh-huh."

"That's good." She sank back against the vinyl booth safely out of his reach.

Damn. That was all he was going to get? One slight touch of her lips?

Not enough. Not nearly enough.

He had to take some kind of action to ensure he would see her often during his month-long stay in Seattle. He wanted Meggie to give him a chance. He wanted to see if he could spark the same feelings without benefit of that confounded disguise.

A simple plan came to him.

He told her about his trouble with the taxi driver who had taken him the long route to the hotel, how his briefcase had been stolen. He embellished the story, playing on her sympathies.

"I feel like such a small-town hick. I want to go sightseeing while I'm in Seattle, but I'm worried about making more mistakes and getting taken advantage of. I feel like a fish out of water."

"You're not as helpless as all that." She laughed and the sound burst through him like a song.

"I am. I'm pathetic in the city."

"No, you're not."

"I swear it. I get lost just crossing the street. Call me a backcountry boy, but I've spent my life with moose and bear and salmon and trees. I don't know much about navigating traffic or getting the best deal at the fish market or how to spot a con artist. Come on, Megs. You gotta take pity on me. I'm begging you. I need someone savvy to show me the city or I'll be stuck in my hotel room for a month."

Her smile broadened. "Why, Caleb, that's an excellent idea."

"It is?" His heart soared and his grin matched hers.

"And have I got just the woman to escort you around town."

He felt confused. Was she talking about herself? "You do?"

"Uh-huh. My best friend, Wendy. She's in between jobs right now and she'd love to show you Seattle. Here, let me give you her phone number."

10

MEGGIE RUMMAGED in her purse for a pen and paper to jot down Wendy's phone number, then looked up and ran smack into Caleb's deep-blue eyes.

He placed one of his large hands over hers. The warmth, and the corresponding jolt of awareness, surprised her as much as the odd expression on his face. She felt flustered, knocked off balance by his unexpected touch.

"I'm sure your friend Wendy is a terrific woman, but I was hoping that *you* could show me around."

"Oh."

She blinked, not certain what to say next, not really sure what she was feeling. She wished Caleb would take his hand back. The weight of it against her fingers was disconcerting.

"That is, if you don't have other plans. I don't want to intrude."

"No, I have no plans." She stared, owl eyed, uncertain of this strangeness stretching between them.

Caleb couldn't be asking her out. Could he?

Come on, why would she even suppose that? He was her friend, her buddy, the guy she used to babysit when he was still stuffing tadpoles in his pocket. He just wanted someone to hang out with, and here she was blowing it all out of proportion.

She shook her head to dispel her crazy thoughts. What was the matter with her? Had rediscovering her sexual prowess gone to her head?

Imagine. A handsome, rich, younger man like Caleb interested in her? Simply ridiculous.

It had been a very strange forty-eight hours. She was still hungover from her night of sinful luxury with Don Juan, and she was misreading things. That had to be the answer to her confusion.

''Nothing against your friend, Megs. It's just that over the past few months I've grown tired of the dating scene and I just wanted someone I could kick back and relax with. Do you realize that in the past four months I've been on sixty-seven first dates?''

''You're kidding.''

''I wish I were. Frankly, it's exhausting, having to make idle chitchat with someone you don't have anything in common with. Especially for a guy who spends most of his time communing with flora and fauna. And, believe me, most of the women I've met are not the type to sit and watch glaciers melt.''

Why would they be watching glaciers melt when they could eyeball the likes of Caleb's handsome physique?

''No second dates?''

He shook his head. ''Not a one.''

''But why not?''

''It never felt right.''

''Oh.''

''So you don't mind spending a few hours a week dragging a greenhorn tourist around Seattle?'' he asked.

"With you, Caleb, I could spend twenty-four hours a day." Now why had she said that?

Jeez, what was happening to her? She had no idea receiving oral sex from a sexy masked man could so disorient a woman. She had to stop thinking about Don Juan and cease reading sexual innuendo into something as innocent as an old friend's touch.

"What I mean is," she said, backpedaling, "I'd love to show you my city."

CALEB AND MEGGIE STROLLED through the bustling Saturday afternoon crowd at Pike Place Market. The cool autumn breeze rolled in off Puget Sound, carrying with it the earthy aroma of fish and salty sea air. The day was unexpectedly sunny, and behind them, Mount Rainier was visible over the top of the city's skyline.

Meggie was dressed warmly in woolen leggings, a vivid red tunic sweater that complemented her dark hair and ivory complexion, stylish thick-heeled black boots and a black leather jacket. A crimson tam was cocked jauntily on her head, the color reminding him of the bustier she'd worn at the *Metropolitan* party.

He had on black jeans, a black turtleneck and a green-plaid mackinaw. Meggie teased him about the mackinaw, joking that you could take the man out of Alaska but you couldn't take Alaska out of the man. But Caleb saw plenty of other guys dressed as ruggedly as he.

Although a thriving metropolis, Seattle had managed to hang on to its wilderness roots. Things were a bit more casual here then in classy New York or hip L.A. If he were forced to live in a big city in the lower forty-eight, Seattle would be the one he'd choose.

The city, he decided, was a lot like Meggie herself, an interesting mix of sophisticate and earth mother.

A wide array of vendors had their wares spread out in a smorgasbord of selections, from fish to fresh fruits and vegetables to spices and cheese. Tantalizing aromas assaulted their noses.

Also interspersed between the buildings and food stalls were artisans with handmade crafts on display. Leather belts and wallets. Beaded rugs and pottery. Portraits and seascapes. Sculpture and jewelry.

"I come here almost every Saturday morning." Meggie inhaled deeply. "I love the fresh food."

"How about we pick up something for dinner and I cook for you?" Caleb offered. "To thank you for showing me a good time."

"You don't have to do that. We can just grab a pizza and rent a video or something."

His heart skipped a beat. So she had planned for their outing to extend into the evening. This was a good thing. A very, very good thing.

"How about linguine with clam sauce?" he suggested enticingly. "Garlic bread and a tossed salad."

"Okay." She laughed. "You're on."

They wandered through the buildings, picking out the ingredients for their meal. When she casually linked her arm through his, Caleb almost stopped breathing.

He sneaked surreptitious glances her way, trying to decipher what the gesture meant, but she seemed so tranquil he could only conclude she felt relaxed enough in his presence that she hadn't giving a second thought to slipping her arm through his.

Was that a bad sign or a good one?

Meggie chatted gaily about the market, about Seattle, about her job and his lecture series. He hung on her every word, but he was so dazzled by the feel of her arm against his side and the heavenly smell of her that he forgot what she said the minute the words left her ripe, sweet mouth.

She purchased a sack of tangerines from a fruit vendor and, as they strolled, peeled one with her long, slender fingers. Dropping the scalped peel into her sack, she then broke off a segment of the citrus fruit and slipped a wedge into her mouth.

"Mmm."

Her soft sound jolted him straight back to that night at the Claremont Hotel. A shiver sliced through Caleb at the vivid memory.

"Oh, this is *so* good."

Helplessly, he dropped his gaze to her mouth and spotted a glistening bead of wet nectar clinging to her lush bottom lip.

That tiny droplet mesmerized him more surely than a pocket watch entranced a hypnosis enthusiast. And his agony didn't end there. When her tongue darted out and whisked the luscious liquid away, the sight reminded him even more of the erotic adventures they'd shared.

"Here, you've gotta taste this." Meggie stopped walking, reached up and lifted a section of tangerine to his mouth.

With an indrawn breath, Caleb allowed his lips to part. Meggie slipped the tangy, sweet, pulpy fruit between his teeth. Her fingertip, soft and inviting, lightly caressed his lower lip, and Caleb's mouth exploded in a riot of sensation. Between the sugary burst of tangerine on his taste buds and the lingering imprint of Meggie's warm finger on his lips, he seriously considered that he might have just died and gone to heaven. The sound of appreciation he made had nothing to do with the fruit and everything to do with Meggie's closeness.

She beamed at him. ''It's a perfect tangerine, isn't it?''

''Perfect,'' he agreed.

''Want another?''

Baby, you can feed me tangerines all day long, was what he wanted to say, but instead he said, ''Nah, I don't want to fill up before dinner.''

''Okay, but you're missing out.'' She polished off the tangerine with a satisfied smirk, and then daintily licked her fingers in a casual move so frigging hot it left Caleb aching to kiss her to taste the heady flavor of Meggie mixed with the perfect tangerine.

They continued walking. A couple of times she paused and tilted her head, looking at him as if he was a familiar pair of slippers or a comfy bathrobe.

That thought disturbed him. He didn't want to be comfortable and familiar. He wanted to be a dangerous, exciting risk taker like Don Juan.

But he shouldn't be complaining. For now, he had her all to himself. His real self. Not the consummate lover he pretended to be when he was behind that mask.

Ah. The sticking point. Would Meggie rather be with him or some long-dead lothario that Caleb had resurrected in order to romance the woman of his dreams?

Things were getting way too complicated.

He should come clean and tell her the truth about Don Juan, but he didn't know how to start. Besides, he wasn't sure she was ready to hear the truth, and he couldn't bear the thought of losing her friendship.

Meggie leaned her head against his shoulder in a guileless gesture that captured his heart. She pointed to a vendor selling porcelain figurines.

"Ooh, dolls. Let's go see."

Okay. All right. He wouldn't tell her about Don Juan. Not yet, even though he was bursting with the need to scoop her into his arms and kiss her.

He would wait. He would slowly romance her, as Caleb. By the time she realized her true feelings for him, he hoped she would be ready to discover the identity of her mystery lover.

Caleb swallowed hard. He didn't feel particularly good about his plan, but saw no way around it. The outcome hinged on what he did in the next few weeks. Could he get her to see him as boyfriend potential? Could he convince her that she would rather have him than Don Juan?

He had less than four weeks to win her heart. The clock was ticking.

CALEB SEEMED DIFFERENT and Meggie couldn't quite put her finger on why. Usually whenever she was around him she felt as relaxed as she did around her own family, but ever since his arrival in Seattle, there was an odd uneasiness between them.

When she'd leaned in close to feed him that slice

of tangerine, she'd felt his whole body tense, and when her fingers grazed his lip she could have sworn she saw his skin pale.

Was he angry with her for some reason? Meggie had no idea why. She glanced over at him. The afternoon sun had slipped from behind the ever-present clouds, catching them for a moment in a swathe of orange light.

His hair glinted darkly. A five-o'clock shadow had begun to sprout on his rugged jaw. His brow was pulled down in a brooding expression. His eyes, as blue as the ocean beyond the pier, shimmered with an intensity that grabbed hold of her belly and squeezed. In that moment, he was a complete stranger to her.

Meggie gulped and the oddest sensation came over her. She couldn't begin to name her emotion. Anxiety maybe, but a nicer feeling than that. Apprehension? No, not really. She wasn't afraid of Caleb.

Excitement? Weirdly enough there was an element of that. Fondness? She'd always been fond of Caleb, but the sensation was deeper, more complex, than fondness.

Knocked off balance by the abnormal emotion—whatever it was—Meggie shook her head and hung back.

Caleb stopped and turned to look at her. The crowd flowed around them, but it was as if they were the only two people in the marketplace. The sun was retreating into the clouds, but left behind enough light to silhouette him in a surreal, ethereal glow.

He looked like…who?

Meggie stopped breathing as a dark, unthinkable

thought skittered across her consciousness, but she quickly shoved it aside before it had time to take root in her head and bloom.

She needed something to distract her. Now.

The dolls. That was the answer. They'd been on their way to look at the doll vendor's stand. With her blood darting rapidly through her veins, she hurried over to the vendor without glancing in Caleb's direction again.

Inexplicably, her hand trembled slightly as she picked up a doll and pretended to examine it. But, in truth, she couldn't seem to focus on the porcelain figurine in her hand.

Calm down, Meggie. What's wrong with you?

She felt Caleb come up behind her and stand so close he almost touched her. Meggie's body flooded with a sharp rush of adrenaline. She had the wildest urge to either flee or spin on her heels and snap at him to back away.

The fight or flight response.

But why on earth was she experiencing that cornered-animal gut reaction to a man she had known her entire life? It made absolutely no sense.

Was she *attracted* to Caleb Greenleaf?

At once, she knew it was true. When the switch had been flipped, she couldn't say, but she wasn't about to let Caleb know of her feelings. He was her ex-stepbrother, for crying out loud. He was two-and-a-half years her junior, and Meggie had no doubt that he considered her nothing more than a friend.

Whoa! Slow down. What is going on with you, Meggie? So what if you're attracted to Caleb? It means nothing. Probably just some temporary tran-

sitional thing you're going through. Like when patients fall in love with their therapists. Displacement. That was it.

Okay. She was calming down. *See? Deep breath in, deep breath out. Calm. Controlled.*

She was attracted to Caleb because he was familiar. He had been kind to her. And this probably had something to do with Don Juan stirring up a lot of sensual feelings she'd kept buried for a long time. Her unexpected desire for Caleb was simply a result of her rebounding femininity. This would pass.

"See anything you like?" Caleb murmured, his warm breath fanning the hairs on the nape of her neck.

Meggie forced herself not to shiver. She started to shake her head, but then her gaze landed on a black porcelain mask. A glass miniature of the same type of mask Don Juan had worn. She reached out to touch the mask in the bizarre hope of grounding herself.

"Ah, you're attracted to the unknown," the doll vendor said. She was a gray-haired woman with an unlined face and mystic aura about her. She wore a dreamy, blue gauze dress and too much jewelry.

"What?" Meggie blinked.

"The mask. It represents what we keep hidden deep within us. The veil that separates the civilized part of our psyche from the uncivilized. The mask symbolizes our secret desires, our forbidden passions, our clandestine affairs."

A coldness passed through Meggie. It was as if the woman possessed a strange telepathy that allowed her to look straight into her heart.

"We'll take it," Caleb told the woman.

"No, please. I can't let you buy this for me." Meggie shook her head.

"You like it and I want to get you something to repay you for squiring me around town."

"Showing you Seattle is my pleasure."

"We'll take it," he repeated insistently, and pulled a wad of cash from his pocket.

"Caleb." Meggie leaned back against his body to whisper a warning. "Don't be such a tourist. This isn't Bear Creek. Don't go flashing your money."

His face colored and he looked chagrined. He peeled off two twenties and handed them to the doll vendor to cover the cost of the mask, then stuffed his money clip back into his front pocket.

Meggie realized she'd embarrassed him and immediately felt bad. "I'm sorry to make a fuss," she mumbled.

"Don't be," he said. "You were absolutely right."

The doll vendor wrapped up his purchase, made change and handed him the sack. He turned the package over to Meggie. "To mark the event of my visit to Seattle."

She clutched the sack to her chest, felt the solid weight of the mask inside the package correspond with the solid lump of emotion lodged in her chest.

"Thank you. It's a lovely gift and awfully sweet of you to buy it for me."

Their eyes met. Something meaningful passed between them. Something more than mere friendship. Something she was too afraid to name.

"You're welcome."

He smiled, and for one starstruck moment she thought he was going to touch her face, but instead he clapped his palms together. ''Now how about we get those ingredients for that clam sauce?''

TWO HOURS LATER they were ensconced in Meggie's apartment, with a crackling fire in her gas fireplace and a feast laid out across the dining room table.

They had prepared dinner together, chopping and mixing, slicing and dicing, stirring and sautéing. They'd sipped wine as they worked, and Caleb had fiddled with the dial on her radio, jumping from station to station until he caught an edgy salsa beat and left it tuned there.

They had bopped around the kitchen to the lively tunes while the exotic Spanish sound brought unbidden thoughts of Don Juan. Would she ever see her mysterious lover again? Did she even want to?

But she pushed those questions aside to listen to Caleb talk about the lectures, his impression of Seattle and what tourist attraction he wanted to see next.

A fissure of pleasure broke through her earlier anxiety because things seemed to have gone back to normal between her and Caleb.

They were friends again and nothing more.

Thank heavens.

Meggie discounted the weird flush of emotions she'd felt at the Pike Place Market, chalking everything up to her fascination with Don Juan. She was so intrigued by the man she was imagining the most ridiculous things. She really had to do something about her obsession with Don Juan before it started causing her serious problems.

''This clam sauce is the best I've ever tasted,''

Meggie told Caleb, determined not to think of Don Juan for the rest of the evening.

He grinned at her. "Thanks."

"You're going to make some lucky lady a very good husband someday."

"You think?"

"Oh, absolutely."

She waved a hand. She was feeling a little tipsy from the wine. A soft, warm glow settled over her. She was happy to be sitting here with her friend, and she was glad he hadn't let her fix him up with Wendy. While she had boiled the linguini, he'd set the table and lit the candles that had been sitting on her dining room table for years. When she looked at him across the table, she saw twin candle flames reflected in his eyes.

"For the life of me, Caleb, I don't know why some woman hasn't already snapped you up."

He shrugged. "Guess I just haven't met the right one yet."

Why *wasn't* he married yet? The man was beyond gorgeous. And kind and trustworthy and wealthy and very, very sexy.

As far as she knew he'd never even had a serious relationship. Quinn had mentioned once that Caleb had sown a few wild oats in college, but no one in Bear Creek could ever recall him having a steady girlfriend.

Why not? He didn't seem like a one-night stand kind of guy.

Yeah, and seven weeks ago you weren't a one-night stand kind of girl.

She thought of Don Juan again, felt a flush of heat rise to her face.

Dammit! She was not going to think about him anymore. The affair was over and that's the way she wanted it.

''Let me speculate,'' she said, looking for any excuse to distract herself. ''You're a wee bit commitment phobic because of your family history.''

''On the money.'' Caleb gave her a wry smile. ''When your mother has been married three times and your father twice, and you have a total of eleven stepsiblings or half siblings, it sorta shakes your faith in happily ever after.''

''Tell me about it.'' Meggie shook her head.

''You're thinking of Jesse.''

''Well, we were together six years.''

''How come you married him, Megs? If you don't mind me asking.''

''I messed up. What can I say?''

''Was it an opposites-attract kind of thing between you two? Or did you have that silly romantic notion women sometimes get, thinking they can change the bad boy? Because I never understood what you saw in him and I always thought you deserved better.''

''My, my. What a big speech for a guy who doesn't talk much,'' Meggie teased, but the hitch in her stomach made it hard to breathe.

''I won't get offended if you tell me it's none of my damned business. Because it's not. But I'm curious.''

Meggie stared into her wineglass and took a swig of the tepid liquid. ''To tell you the truth, I've been struggling to answer that question myself.''

"Come up with any stunning insight?"

He cocked his head to one side. In that moment he looked so endearingly boyish, Meggie felt something warm and slippery melt inside her.

"Other than I was young and dumb?"

"Yeah, other than that." He grinned.

Caleb made her feel safe. Like she could tell him anything and it would be all right. She recalled then pleasant snippets from their childhood. Because of his jumbled family life, Caleb had often stayed with the Scofields, especially during the summer when school was out and his stepsiblings had shuttled off in a half-dozen different directions on vacations with their respective parents. Homebody Caleb had always preferred staying in Bear Creek, and Meggie's loving parents had readily opened their home to him.

They'd had the kind of routine that had stayed with her as a model of how summer mornings were suppose to be. As kids, they rose early, listening to the birds trilling. They'd make themselves breakfast if her parents were still asleep. Cold cereal or frozen waffles if Meggie convinced the boys to eat properly. Cookie dough or leftover pizza or even ice cream if they had their way.

Then her parents would get up. Usually her father first, shuffling into the kitchen in his bathrobe to make coffee while her mother showered. Then her mom would make them a picnic lunch if they were going exploring. Cheese and bread, fruit and juice that she put in brown paper sacks. She'd wave them off with instructions not to get lost or fall into the fjord.

"Remember when we were kids and you used to spend the summer with Quinn?"

"I remember."

"You guys were nice to let me tag along with you, even though I was such a cautious scaredy-cat."

"I think your mother made us."

"Yeah, well, there was that." She smiled at him. "But somewhere along the way, I picked up this craving for adventure. Funny, though. At the very same time I was always afraid of letting go, of being out of control."

"You're a complicated lass, Meggie Scofield."

She laughed. "That's one way of looking at it."

"So what did Jesse have to do with any of this?"

Meggie moistened her lips. "Okay, here it is. My theory on why I was with your stepbrother."

Caleb pushed his plate aside, propped his elbows on the table and dropped his chin into his open palms. "I'm all ears. Go on."

"The way I figure it, with my limited knowledge of pop psychology, Jesse provided me with a safe outlet, a way to get my vicarious thrills. I could watch him skydive or bungee jump and I never had to take a risk or put myself out there. I inhaled the fumes from his high and that got me by. Secondhand adventure, so to speak. Does that make any sense?"

Caleb nodded. "I can see where you might find my stepbrother exciting."

"Also makes sense that he would eventually leave me for being too dull."

"You're not dull," he declared vehemently. "Not in the least."

"Oh, believe me, I was. I spent all my time working. My job is everything to me. I never wanted to try anything new, do anything different. I had my routine and I liked things that way. I've got to thank Jesse for that at least. He shook me up and made me realize how I'd been sleepwalking through life."

"If you say so."

"But that's all changed now. I've starting taking a few risks of my own and I'm amazed at what I've discovered about myself."

"How? What happened?"

Meggie ducked her head, suddenly embarrassed. Should she tell him about Don Juan?

"Megs?"

She raised her chin and met his gaze. She saw nothing but calm acceptance reflected in those big blue eyes. Maybe if she told him about Don Juan she could start getting over her obsession with the fantasy.

Caleb was a great listener and an even better friend. He wouldn't go back to Bear Creek and gossip. If she told him about Don Juan, no one else would ever find out.

"I've got big ears and tight lips."

"Your ears aren't big." She swatted playfully at his shoulder, almost fell out of her chair and realized belatedly she was a tad tipsy.

"Whoa there." He put out a hand to steady her and his touch did very strange things to her skin. It sizzled, fizzled and tingled.

It's just the wine, ninny.

"Thank you, kind sir."

Caleb's eyebrows dipped in a frown. "Are you okay?"

Gosh, he seemed so serious. Meggie hiccuped, lifted a palm to her mouth and giggled. "Oops, sorry."

''Don't feel embarrassed around me. How long have we known each other?''

''Years and years and years.''

Man, he really was cute, especially when you focused on his perfect mouth.

Meggie narrowed her eyes and stared unabashedly at his lips. Gee. His mouth looked a lot like Don Juan's. She must have a thing for really great mouths.

''Exactly. So you should feel free to say anything to me. Anything in the world.''

''Anything?''

She would bet her last quarter that wasn't really true. What would he do if she told him she thought she might be developing a serious crush on his mouth? And that she was fighting the strongest urge to kick off her sneakers, run her toes up his shin and play a down-and-dirty game of footsie?

Ha! He'd probably make a human-size hole in the wall as he ran away from her.

''Anything,'' he reiterated.

''Okay, then. I think I've had too much wine.''

''All right.'' He took her glass away. ''Is there anything else you want to tell me?''

Damn, he seemed to know something was gnawing at her, and he obviously wasn't going to let it lie. Served her right for knowing him more than half her life.

''Meggie, it's me, Caleb. You know you can trust me with your darkest secrets.''

He reached out and squeezed her hand, giving her the courage to spill out her heart and ask his advice on how to stop fixating on yet another bad boy.

That did it. The giddiness of the wine, the warmth

of this hand and her desperate desire to overcome her sexual obsession all culminated into one unstoppable urge to come clean about what she had been up to with that dastardly Don Juan.

"Caleb," she whispered, "I've got something to confess."

11

ONE SECOND. Two. Three. Was she going to tell him about Don Juan?

''Why don't we go sit in front of the fire?'' she invited with a coy little smile that jerked his heart-strings. ''Get comfortable.''

''Okay.'' He held out his palm. She hesitated only the briefest second before sinking her hand into his and allowing him to lead her into the living room area.

He wanted to kiss her so badly he couldn't think, but he had to be careful, had to move slowly. When he'd bought her the mask this afternoon and she'd acted so oddly he thought maybe he'd already ruined everything. But tonight, preparing the meal together, and just now, when she'd agreed to tell him her darkest secret, Caleb felt the old sense of camara-derie return.

He also felt a nasty stab of guilt. Because she was tipsy, she was about to entrust him with her vulner-ability, and he was the one lying to her. Should he stop her before she got started?

God forgive him, but he couldn't. He had to hear what she was going to say.

They sat crossed-legged on the rug in front of the fire. Meggie pushed her hair back from her face.

Lord, she was lovely. She leaned her head against his shoulder and sighed contentedly. The weight of her against him caused a sweet ache in his soul.

Her lashes drifted half-shut as she stared at the mesmerizing flames. Caleb's anxiety mounted with each passing moment that she didn't speak, but he was not going to rush her.

Finally she said, "I met this guy."

Struggling to maintain a cool facade, he simply nodded.

She gave him a sideways glance, as if gauging his reaction, and seemed reassured. She told him then about how she'd met Don Juan at the *Metropolitan* party, how she didn't even know his name but she'd recklessly given him her phone number. How he'd turned up in Seattle for one glorious night.

"He's so wrong for me, but I'm afraid I'm hooked."

Caleb pursed his lips but said nothing.

"Don't get me wrong. I'm not thinking of this guy as happily ever after material. Not by a long shot."

"No?"

"Honestly, I'm not. I didn't want anything more from him than great sex."

"Megs, this falls under the category of a little too much information."

"I've embarrassed you. I was afraid of that. You still see me as an older sister figure, and here I am talking about sex."

"I'm not embarrassed," he growled. *And the last thing I see you as is my sister.* "Keep talking."

"You sure?"

"Positive. I told you I'm here for you, no matter what."

"Okay. Like I was saying, the last thing I want is any kind of a relationship with this guy."

Caleb didn't know what to think about this latest development. Or how to feel. He wanted her to want him, not Don Juan. But if she just wanted Don Juan for sex, what did that mean for him?

Damn. This whole deception was turning into a real mess. What had started out as a daring game had veered into dangerous territory.

"This guy is just a bit of the hair of the dog, if you know what I mean. I suppose I'm using him to get this wildness out of my system, to boost my ego. Doesn't that sound terrible? Using a guy for sex."

"Not if it's what you need."

"And it seems to be working."

"Does it?"

"Well, except for one thing."

"Yes?"

God, what a struggle to keep his tone noncommittal and not say anything that might do irreparable damage to their friendship.

"I'm completely obsessed with him," she whispered.

He looked into her eyes, two glorious green vortexes shimmering with the seductive double whammy of shame and thrill. Her upper teeth sank into her full lower lip, and Meggie dipped her head a bit to hide her expression from his perusal.

Her confession caught him by surprise, while at the same time filled his heart with an inexplicable joy. Meggie was obsessed with him!

Not you, dimwit. She's obsessed with a fantasy. When she finds out the truth, she's gonna be mightily pissed off.

"I can't stop thinking about him. I know it's foolish, but there it is." She knotted her fingers and dropped her hands into her lap.

"It's just an infatuation."

"I know. And even if it wasn't, I realize this guy's not right for me. I know nothing about him, and besides, how could a relationship built solely on sex ever stand a chance?"

"Do you want a real relationship with him?" Caleb dared to ask.

"No." She shook her head vehemently. "I just wish I could stop thinking about him."

"It's the mystery that's intrigued you. That's all."

"You're absolutely right and that's what I keep telling myself. I'm betting if I were to meet this guy without his mask and costume I wouldn't be attracted to him in the slightest."

Ouch. That wasn't pleasant to hear. The whole Don Juan thing was backfiring on him. In the beginning, Caleb's rationale for hiding behind the disguise was to convince Meggie to see him as a virile, potent man who desired her.

What had started as an impetuous impulse upon meeting Klondike Kate had turned into a driving desire to indulge his long-held fantasies, once he'd discovered who she was.

He recalled the first time he had became aware of Meggie as a woman. It was the summer he was fourteen and she was sixteen. She'd shown up to go sailing with him and Jesse and Quinn, wearing white short-shorts and a blue polka-dot halter top. He could still remember how the soft material had clung to her breasts. How he'd been completely fascinated by the sight.

He swallowed hard. He was slipping, sliding, tumbling headlong to a place he wasn't sure he wanted to go because it was simply too overwhelming. And the realization that he wanted more from her, that two nights of anonymous sex were never going to be enough for him, scared the living hell out of Caleb.

What did it all mean?

"It's getting late and the rain is drumming pretty hard on the roof," he said, unnerved by the thoughts and memories rushing through his head. "I should go."

"You don't have to leave."

"No?" He looked at her, and she was giving him a smile that was quintessential Meggie. His heart tripped. What was she implying?

"The couch makes into a bed," she said, dashing his foolish hopes that she'd meant something else. "I keep an extra toothbrush in the cupboard in case of company."

The idea of staying the night was incredibly tempting. Too damned tempting. He thought of lying on the couch while she slept in the next room, and he knew he'd never be able to do it.

"I think I better go. I have some paperwork to catch up on."

"Oh, okay."

She walked him to the door. They stood there a minute looking at each other.

"What I told you tonight was strictly confidential," she said.

"Of course."

"Thanks, Caleb. It helped, talking to you about my little, er...problem."

"Anytime."

She rose up on her toes, leaned in and planted a kiss on his cheek. "You're the greatest."

"See you tomorrow?" he asked.

She shook her head. "I've got to work and then I've got a committee meeting."

"Monday?"

"I've got belly dancing class."

"Oh."

"But maybe after? We could go to a movie or a comedy club or check out a local band."

"Sounds good." He didn't care where he went or what he did as long as Meggie was there.

"Why don't you pick me up at the dance studio? My class is over at seven."

The thought of watching Meggie belly dance drove a spike of hot, achy need right through his spine. And the imprint of her lips still burned his cheek, feeding his libido. It was all he could do not to kiss her back, and this time not on the cheek.

She gave him the address of the studio, then ruffled his hair. "Good night, little brother. See ya on Monday."

Caleb left her apartment gritting his teeth and clutching the pink paisley umbrella she had given him, knowing one thing for certain. He would have to take some very determined steps to show Meggie exactly how unbrotherly he could be.

But where and how to start?

He had no idea how to go about seducing her without that damnable mask.

MEGGIE SHUT THE DOOR behind Caleb and sagged against it, thankful he'd decided not to stay the night. But she was not really sure why she was so relieved. Probably because she felt pretty darned vulnerable after spilling her guts to him about Don Juan. Why had she told Caleb all that stuff?

Or maybe you're glad he left because of the way he's starting to make you feel, an irritating voice in the back of her mind whispered.

Frowning, Meggie began putting their dinner dishes in the dishwasher. That was ridiculous. She wasn't feeling any differently toward Caleb than she ever had.

Oh no? Then why were you noticing how nicely his long legs looked stretched out across your carpet? Why were you admiring the way his dark hair curls around his collar? And I saw you staring at his chiseled-from-granite biceps.

"I wasn't," she retorted, jamming forks, spoons and knives into the silverware holder.

Liar.

What about the way he'd listened to her confession about Don Juan, without a hint of judgment or condemnation on his face?

"So he's a good friend. I already knew that."

You kissed him.

"On the friggin' cheek."

First comes the cheek. The lips are bound to follow.

"Oh, shut up."

She scrubbed her large cooking pot, attacking the starchy linguini residue with a vengeance.

And then you went and invited him to come watch you belly dance. Now tell the truth, what in the hell was that all about?

What indeed?

"This is preposterous," she muttered. "I'm not attracted to Caleb Greenleaf, for heaven's sake."

Why not? This time it was Wendy's voice echoing in her head. *He's handsome and smart and rich. Reliable and trustworthy and kind.*

Why not, indeed?

Meggie rinsed off a dinner plate. Well, for one thing, he had shown absolutely no indication of being interested in her.

He bought you the porcelain mask.

"Big deal. He's a generous guy."

He cooked dinner.

"He was just thanking me for showing him around town."

Why are you showing him around town?

"He's an old friend!"

Yeah, right.

"He is," Meggie stubbornly insisted to herself.

Okay, so why haven't you introduced him to Wendy yet?

"Because he's all wrong for her."

Really? Maybe it's because you think he's all right for you.

"Come on, he's *not* interested in me!"

And even if he was interested in her, which she seriously doubted, Meggie wasn't about to embarrass herself by coming on to a younger man. No way, no how.

I'd rather be an old man's darling than a young man's fool. One of Wendy's favorite reasons for dating older men flitted through her head.

And Meggie was a little gun-shy about taking a risk and laying her emotions on the line, which no doubt explained her interest in her no-strings-attached relationship with Don Juan. With him she didn't have to worry about getting hurt. Caleb, however, was another story completely. Just thinking about Caleb in this strange new way caused her to hyperventilate.

No. Absolutely not.

Meggie cringed, imagining what her mother would say, how the gossip would fly from one corner of Bear Creek to the other.

"We're just friends!" she shouted to the wall. "Nothing's changed."

But in her heart, she wasn't so sure she believed that.

THE DANCE STUDIO was chockful of attractive women, but Caleb had eyes for only one. He was standing outside the door of Meggie's belly dancing class, peering through the glass partition and trying hard to work up the courage to step inside.

So strong was his desire for her, Caleb didn't trust himself not to have an overt physical reaction, and he didn't want to embarrass them both in public with a gigantic erection.

When had he lost control over his own body? What was it about Meggie that caused him to act like a horny teenager in the throes of a hormonal storm?

He watched greedily as she undulated in the middle of the room with the other dancers. She wore a gauzy little *I Dream of Jeannie* outfit that showed far too much of her smooth flat belly.

She was the most conspicuous woman in the room, moving with the grace of a true performer. Her arms were raised over her head as she clicked tiny cymbals attached to her fingers. She turned with the group, but she was much more graceful than the others. She was facing away from him now, rolling those curvaceous hips as if she were personally beckoning him to her.

Come.

God, she was hot!

Shake it, baby. The crude, yet thoroughly masculine thought bounced through his brain. He felt like a voyeur, like some kind of a Peeping Tom pervert, but he simply could not stop himself from watching…and wishing she was performing this erotic dance just for him. He hated the thought that anyone else might see her and lust after her.

He realized he was jealous and there was no one to be jealous of. The room contained only the other dancers and the female instructor. No one else was peeking through the glass partition with him.

Cricket on a crutch! He was in deep, and like a quicksand victim, the harder he struggled the deeper he sank. He was falling for her. Fast.

And the misguided jealousy streaking through his heart told him he couldn't fool himself any longer. The desire he felt for her went far beyond the physical. He'd been kidding himself when he decided making love to Meggie would once and forever quell his sexual fantasies about her.

What an idiot he'd been, thinking he could take this lightly and then just walk away.

Meggie executed a series of complicated shifts and steps that had Caleb almost swallowing his tongue. He found his own body swaying in time to the seductive Middle Eastern music seeping under the door and oozing out into the corridor. A mesmerizing sound that had him aching to dance with her. To press her body against his as they moved in tandem.

Stupid urge. He had no idea how to dance.

And yet here he was, his hands burning to touch that wavering waist, to grind his pelvis against those incredible, womanly hips.

The costume she wore was almost as provocative as the scintillating dance she performed. The silky material clung to her well-developed curves and rippled with a stimulating flow that incited his hormones to riot. And a filmy purple veil cloaked her mouth, hiding those full lips he loved so much and adding a tantalizing layer of mystery to her dance.

God, she was gorgeous. The memory of her scent came to him, clinging to his nostrils as surely as if she were standing next to him—the sweet, erotic elixir of lavender, strawberries and Obsession. He recalled the taste of her as well—hot, rich, creamy.

If he wasn't careful he was going to start salivating right there on the spot.

He realized his palms were pressed against the

glass, his eyes trained on her. He was a kid outside a toy store with no money in his pockets.

Why had she invited him here?

The thought struck him from the blue and the answer came to him.

This was another one of her fantasies, entitled Just Watch Me, or Let Me Drive You Wild. She was playing a game. Teasing and tantalizing him. But he didn't think she'd been consciously aware of what she was doing when she had encouraged him to come by and pick her up. In fact, he knew that if he were to point out this astounding fact to her, not only would she deny it but she would probably get defensive.

This sudden insight into her psyche jerked like a string attached to his heart. There was only one reason why her subconscious would prod her to ask him to come to the dance studio so he would see her performing such a rousing routine in that electrifying costume. On some uncharted subterranean level she wanted *him.*

A surge of hope, more uplifting than he thought possible, rose inside him. A powerful updraft of expectancy that said yes, maybe he stood a chance of winning her over on his own—without that damned mask.

The music ended. Caleb shook his head, breaking from his reverie as he realized the dance class was over. The door opened and women began streaming out.

Meggie was the last one through the door, and the minute she spotted him, her face lit up with a smile that twinkled like the myriad of holiday decorations the Scofields had put up around their house every winter when he and Meggie were kids. His own parents had been too busy marrying and divorcing to bother much with Christmas ornamentation.

Her excited expression underscored his hope. Caleb was jubilant. He wanted to dance a jig right there in the hallway with her classmates streaming around them. He wasn't wrong on this matter and he knew it, even if Meggie wasn't yet ready to admit to herself what game she was playing.

Did she suspect, at least on a subconscious level, that he was indeed Don Juan?

"Caleb!" She thrust herself into his arms for a quick hug.

The gossamer material of her outfit grazed his hand and spent a spark of awareness leaping up his nerve endings. She smelled of sweet perspiration and earthy woman, a scent that drove him to the very brink of distraction.

She stepped back. "Have you been here long?"

"A few minutes."

She lowered her lashes, dabbed at her neck with a small, white gym towel. "Did you see me dance?"

Ah, coyness. This *was* a mating game, whether she would admit it or not.

What a rush.

"I saw you." His tone was sexier than he intended, but dammit, he couldn't help himself.

She lifted her head. Her green eyes were startled, her pupils wide.

She honestly doesn't realize what she's doing to me. This is all subconscious.

"You're very good," he said.

"Thank you. I really love to dance."

"You could be a professional."

"Nah. I'm a nurse at heart, but dancing is my passion."

"I remember."

"You do?"

Caleb stuffed his hands in his front pockets, mainly to keep himself from touching her. His fingers itched to trace the fabric of that sparkly costume and feel her body heat beneath.

"One year for your birthday—I think you were probably eight or nine—your mom got you that pink ballerina outfit and you spent the whole summer twirling up and down the streets of Bear Creek. I recall thinking you looked just like a stick of cotton candy."

And, boy, how he loved cotton candy. He'd been stone-cold addicted to the stuff.

"You remember that? But you were only, what? Six, maybe seven?"

"I remember a lot of things, Meggie."

She seemed flustered. Her cheeks darkened and she glanced away again, jerking a thumb in the direction of a door marked Ladies' Locker Room.

"Listen, I'm going to go hit the showers and change. I'll be ready to leave in about twenty minutes. Is that okay?"

He motioned to a nearby bench positioned beneath a bulletin board. "I don't mind waiting. I'll just have a seat. Take your time."

"You're a doll."

She reached over to ruffle his hair in her irritatingly familiar fashion, but halfway to his head, she seemed to realize what she was doing, stopped and dropped her arm. Without another word, she turned and scurried into the locker room.

Grinning, he settled himself on the bench. *Mark this day on the calendar, folks.* Meggie Scofield had stopped ruffling his hair. One small step in the direction he wanted her to go, but it wasn't enough. He wanted to move faster. He needed a major weapon in his campaign to persuade Meggie to stop seeing him as just an old childhood friend and start picturing him as a potential lover.

What would it take to convince her?

He leaned his head back and collided with the bulletin board behind him. A pushpin fell from the cork, bounced off his head and skittered across the floor. An orange flyer swooped through the air and slid under the bench.

Caleb got up, retrieved the pushpin and fished under the bench for the flyer. He moved to tack it back to the bulletin board, but as he read the page, he stopped and an idea took shape.

> SALSA CLASSES START FRIDAY.
> Looking for an exciting new way to romance your ladylove? Try salsa dancing. She'll be putty in your hands, guaranteed. Even if you've never danced a day in your life, our instructors, the renowned flamenco dancers Raul Roman and his lovely wife Luisa will have you doing the tango, the merengue, the cumbia and many more in a matter of ten easy lessons. Sign up in the office today!

Caleb stared at the flyer. It was as if the thing had been conjured up by divine intervention. He was looking for an exciting new way to romance his lady. And Meggie loved to dance.

Salsa dancing. It was the perfect solution to his dilemma.

Resolutely he pinned the flyer back to the bulletin board and went in search of the office.

12

WHY WAS HER PULSE hammering so hard? Meggie wondered as she stripped out of her belly dancing outfit and stepped into the shower.

Er…maybe because you spent the last fifty minutes belly dancing?

Ha! She wished.

Unfortunately, she had a sneaking suspicion her accelerated heart rate had nothing to do with exercise and everything to do with the way Caleb had been staring at her.

Don't be silly. Don't be ridiculous. Caleb wasn't looking at you any differently than he's ever looked at you.

And if by some chance he *was* looking at her differently, it was only because of her sexy costume. He was a normal red-blooded male. She was a skimpily dressed woman with a bare midriff. What did she expect?

She shouldn't have asked him to pick her up at the dance studio, especially on a night they were performing a dress rehearsal for an upcoming competition. What had she been thinking?

Well, on the practical side, the studio was much closer to the Space Needle—where she'd intended on taking him for dinner—than her apartment. But if she were being honest with herself might she not admit that maybe, just maybe, she'd wanted Caleb to see her dancing in costume?

Why?

That was the sixty-four-thousand-dollar question.

She shook her head to dispel the notion and concentrated on soaping down her body. As she scrubbed, she found her thoughts wandering back to Caleb.

He was such a great guy. Too bad he hadn't been able to find the right woman, particularly after all his friends in Bear Creek had paired up with the ladies of their dreams. He had to be feeling left out.

She slid her hands down her body, lathering her belly and beyond. Her skin tingled where she touched. She was glad Caleb had come to Seattle. He had badly needed the vacation, time away from home. And she was happy she'd been able to show him the town. It'd been fun reconnecting with her old friend again.

And then without warning, an image popped into her mind that was anything but platonic. Meggie pictured Caleb right there in the shower with her. His hands were washing the triangle of hair between her legs. He was taking his long masculine fingers and slowly rubbing her in private places, stimulating her to a fevered pitch as she pressed herself into his hard, naked, wet body.

Yikes!

What in the hell was she thinking? Caleb was the guy next door, the kid she'd spent her summers playing hide and seek with. She should not be having these thoughts about him. Caleb simply was not fantasy material.

Oh yeah? I've seen you giving him the once-over. You can't deny he's gorgeous. Admit it, Meggie. Caleb grew up real nice.

"WHERE ARE WE GOING?" Caleb asked as they left the dance studio. He'd just signed up for ten salsa lessons, and he could barely keep from grinning. Was Meggie ever going to be surprised when he took her salsa dancing.

"Seattle's number one tourist attraction."

"Which is?"

"The Space Needle, of course."

"What?"

Balking, he stopped walking. He wasn't sure Meggie knew of his fear of man-made heights, such as tall buildings, and he hated to admit a weakness, but the thought of going up to the Space Needle made his gut torque.

"I made reservations at SkyCity, the revolving restaurant at the Needle. They make a killer Dungeness crab cocktail, and their famous dessert, the Lunar Orbiter, is to die for. Afterward, I thought we could go up on the observation deck and gaze out at the city lights. I haven't been up there in such a long time, I'm really looking forward to tonight."

Caleb looked at her standing in the glow of the light from the dance studio and his heart slipped in his chest. She held her workout bag in one hand and her car keys in the other.

She wore a flowing rust-colored skirt, the hem just skimming the tops of her calf-high, brown leather boots, and a black long-sleeved Lycra top. She had a cream-colored sweater draped over her shoulders. Her short black hair, still damp from her shower, curled enticingly around her face. She had applied fresh lipstick, and a light dusting of mascara to her lashes, enhancing her natural prettiness without overdoing the cosmetics.

She wasn't a raving beauty in the way of models and movie stars, but in his eyes, Meggie was the most gorgeous creature on the face of the earth. Just looking at her changed him in ways he could not verbally express. She made him want to spend less time alone in the wilderness and more time in the world with people. It was a strange sensation for an introvert, and he didn't completely understand his new emotions.

Her smile encompassed her face and her green eyes came alive with excitement. If she wanted to go to the Space Needle, then, by damn, that's where he would go. Phobia or not.

His bravado held until he was faced with climbing into the toothpaste-dispenser-size elevator at the Space Needle. At the entrance, they were greeted by a pleasant attendant who was extolling the virtues of the glass lift to a handful of other visitors.

"Time to face the fear, Greenleaf," he growled.

"What?" Meggie blinked at him.

"All aboard," the attendant announced, unclipping the velvet rope blocking the entrance to the elevator.

Caleb hung back.

"Come on." Meggie smiled and took his hand.

You can do this. There's nothing to be afraid of. It's just an elevator.

He took solace in the feel of Meggie's warm palm

pressed against his, and reluctantly stepped into the small glass cage. The attendant asked them to move farther back in order to make room for more people. Gritting his teeth, Caleb shifted toward the outer glass wall with a vertigo-inducing view of the ground below.

Up, up, up. The elevator moved with a series of jerky clicks. Was the damned thing suppose to be so noisy? It wasn't natural for the scenery to blur so fast.

Take the risk. You can handle it. Not just for Meggie's sake but also to prove to yourself that you're not set in your ways. You can do different things. You can face your fears. You can adjust to life in the city.

Much to his relief they made it to the restaurant without incident. The hostess escorted them onto the rotating dais and they were seated at an intimate table for two with a spectacular view of Seattle.

He felt a little quivery, but took in a deep breath and managed to quell the jitters by gazing into Meggie's face cast so beautifully in candlelight. He wasn't going to let a bad childhood memory control his life.

"Isn't this fabulous?" Meggie enthused, turning her head to look out the window and revealing the smooth expanse of her long, graceful neck.

"Yes," he said.

But much more fabulous than the panorama below was the stunning view right across from him. Meggie beamed at him and he felt as if he'd been given the most precious of gifts.

He did as she suggested and ordered the crab. She chattered gaily and, it seemed, a little nervously, as if frightened to leave the opportunity for silence. Caleb wondered why. He and Meggie had sat in companionable silence many times before. It was one of the things he loved most about her. In the past, she'd waited patiently in the forest with him in the hopes of spotting a mama bear with her cubs or a bald eagle building a nest. Why this sudden need to fill the air with talk?

"What do you think of Seattle?" Meggie asked.

"It's a very romantic place, as far as cities go. Of course, nothing can beat Bear Creek for sheer beauty."

"Romantic?" There was laughter in her voice. "Can't say I've ever thought of Seattle as romantic. Too much darn rain."

"Rain can be sexy."

"Oh?"

"Sure. Like the other night at your apartment. A roaring fire, good company, rain drumming seductively on the roof."

"You thought *that* was romantic? Dear Caleb, you've got to get out more."

"That's why I'm here."

"Is it?"

His gaze met hers. "Yep. I came to Seattle to explore the perimeters of romance."

"Ah, now you're pulling my leg."

"A little," he admitted, enjoying the teasing banter between. "But I confess—I am searching for something."

He waited to see what she would say. He felt sexual chemistry shimmering between them, but he had to wonder if it was all in his imagination.

"Have you found what you're looking for yet?"

"Maybe. I can't say for sure."

"Oh."

He glanced at her. She was slowly scooting her food around on her plate.

"Is something wrong?" he asked.

"No." She shook her head.

"Not still pining over this Don Juan guy?" he dared to inquire.

"Nah," she muttered, but dropped her gaze.

"You've beaten your obsession?"

"Yes. Talking about it with you the other night helped immensely. Thanks."

He wasn't sure that he believed her. Something was different between them and he didn't know what. Or why.

The waiter cleared their dinner plates, brought coffee, two spoons and one serving of the spectacular Lunar Orbiter dessert, which turned out to be a massive ice cream concoction delivered with fanfare amid swirls of dry ice to simulate Seattle fog.

She scooped up a spoonful of ice cream. Caleb's gaze tracked her movements, fixating on her lips as she daintily slid the cold ice cream into her warm, wct mouth.

"Mmm," she moaned, soft and low.

When she flicked out her tongue to whisk away a drop of melted ice cream from her bottom lip, he shivered so hard he felt it straight down through his bones.

"Caleb, are you okay?"

Easy, Greenleaf. You're going to give this gig away before you have a chance to put Operation Salsa Dancing in action.

"Yeah...I—" His voice cracked. "Uh..."

Oh, that was about as smooth as gravel.

She reached out and placed her hand over his. "Is something wrong?"

Other than the fact that her touch was causing him to get a high-voltage hard-on?

"Fine," he lied. "Absolutely fine."

They lingered for a while, talking softly, enjoying the city lights, savoring the dessert. Meggie tried to pay for the meal, and when Caleb refused to let her, she lobbied for dutch treat.

"No," he said adamantly. "This one's on me."

"Okay, I give up. You win. Pay away." She waved a hand.

"Thank you."

"You know, most guys would jump at a chance to let their date pay."

"I'm not most guys."

She studied him with a pensive expression. "No, no, you're not."

"And we're not on a date."

"We aren't, are we?"

"Nope."

Caleb rose to his feet, took her sweater from the back of her chair and held it out for her to slip her arms into. She seemed flustered by the gesture and missed the armhole twice before getting it right.

"Ready to go out on the observation deck?" she asked just a bit too brightly.

"Uh-huh." He didn't want to go, but he wanted to be with Meggie. Anything to prolong this evening. Even if it entailed peering down from a great man-made height.

He gulped.

Meggie guided him from the restaurant and up a short flight of stairs to the observation deck. The minute she took his hand, her heart started the same crazy stuttering it had back in the shower at the dance studio. What on earth was the matter with her? Wrong time of the month maybe?

But of course not. PMS triggered crankiness and cramps, not this strange, inexplicable euphoria that set her heart to skipping beats.

This was Caleb, for crying out loud, not Don Juan. Had her hormones gone haywire?

Disconcerted, she dropped his hand and moved out onto the observation deck. Clutching her sweater more tightly around her in the wind, she meandered to the edge of the railing and stared out into the night.

When Caleb didn't move to join her, she turned to find him still hovering in the archway between the restaurant and the deck.

The sight of him standing there, his hair whipping sexily in the breeze, his coat collar flipped up around his strong, muscular neck, made her feel very mixed up indeed. She had an inexplicable hunger to feel his arms wrapped around her waist. She wanted to lean against his chest, rest her head on his shoulders.

"Come on." She motioned him over.

"I'm fine right here," he called.

"The view is terrific." She pointed. "Come look at the harbor."

"You go ahead."

"What's the matter, Greenleaf? You chicken?"

"Actually, yes."

"You?" She laughed. "I don't believe it."

"Guilty as charged. I'm afraid of heights."

"But you climbed Mount McKinley with Quinn and you serve on the mountain rescue squad."

"I'm not afraid of heights per se. Just man-made heights. Towers, tall buildings that sway, elevators that go farther than ten or twelve floors. It's sort of a claustrophobia-acrophobia combo."

"That's right. I remember Jesse saying something about that. You got lost in an elevator at the Eiffel Tower when you were a kid."

"Lost, my ass. Jesse abandoned me."

"No kidding?"

"No kidding."

"He was suppose to be watching me but instead he got distracted by some girl and let me get into the elevator by myself. Just so happens the elevator hangs up and I'm stuck in there alone for two hours."

"He was an irresponsible butthead even back then."

"Yes, he was."

They smiled at each other.

His admission of vulnerability surprised her. Strong, capable Caleb afraid of something? She would never have imagined it. She thought of Don Juan and what he had shown her about herself. He'd taught her how to take risks, and she would be forever grateful for that lesson.

Meggie extended her hand to Caleb. "I've recently learned a powerful lesson about facing your fears."

"Oh yeah?"

"Yeah."

"And what is that?"

"If you want to find out what you're really made of, you've got to take a few risks. Come on. Join me on the ledge of life.'' She swept a hand at their surroundings. ''I have faith in you.''

''Meggie, you have no idea what a challenge this is for me.''

''But that's wonderful. The bigger the risk, the bigger the payoff.''

''You think so?''

''I know so.''

''Lady, when you throw down a gauntlet, you throw down a gauntlet,'' he grumbled, but even as he shook his head he was slowly edging one foot toward her.

''You'll thank me in the morning.''

''Humph.''

''Come to me,'' she beckoned, wriggling her fingers at him.

He started toward her. The floor beneath them swayed ever so slightly in the gusting wind, and she saw him wince.

''You can do this,'' she coaxed.

''This better be worth it.''

''Trust me. One step at a time.''

And that's how he did it, one step at a time toward the brink. When he finally reached her, his face broke into a smile that stole her heart.

''Woo-ho! You did it.''

''I did it,'' he echoed.

''Congratulations. You conquered your fear of man-made heights,'' she murmured, and spontaneously threw her arms around him.

And then, not even realizing what she had intended on doing, she kissed him.

Caleb wrapped his arms around her as her lips sank

onto his, enveloping her in his woodsy scent. The smell of him entered her nostrils, invaded her bloodstream with a heady rush of sensation.

Heaven help her, she hadn't meant to give him a real kiss. It was just suppose to be an atta-boy-I'm-darned-proud-of-you-for-conquering-your-fear kiss. But somewhere between her lips and his, the intention had become distorted, and she could not seem to control what happened next.

Blame it on Don Juan. Blame it on the full moon. Blame it on the fact that for the first time in her life she was seeing Caleb for who he was now and not for the kid next door he had once been.

He was all-man, absolutely no doubt about it.

Meggie melted against his body. She increased the pressure of the kiss, coaxing his lips apart, thrilling to her own bravery. Caleb wasn't the only one taking risks tonight. She'd never been the aggressor in romance. Had never initiated a first kiss.

Boy, when she let her guard down, she really let her guard down.

Gently, she flicked her tongue over his lips, slow and lazy, seducing him by increments. Her head spun with the realization of her own audacity as she took their first kiss deeper and deeper still.

He tasted of creamy, sweet Lunar Orbiter and strong, dark espresso. And something else. A sweet, familiar taste she could not name.

His mouth was hot and moist against hers. The gusting wind, the tower's gentle sway, shook the very air between their bodies and sent a fog mist swirling about them like something from a fantasy.

Time out! her brain cried. *What do you think you're*

doing? More importantly, what message are you sending Caleb? You're giving him ideas you're not able to support. Wise up, Meggie. Wise up right now.

With a low, throaty moan, he arched his body into hers, and when he reached out a hand and cupped the curve of her hip, Meggie's eyes flew open. He was staring at her and she knew then that she was in over her head. Startled and suddenly frightened by what she had done, Meggie pulled away.

"I—I...didn't mean to do that," she stammered. "Please don't take this the wrong way. I certainly wasn't trying to seduce you."

"You could have fooled me."

His voice was rough, abrupt. Was he angry or disappointed? She couldn't blame him for being either. She'd sort of led him on. But she hadn't meant to. It had just happened.

"I know. I'm sorry." She turned her back, unable to look him in the eyes. Oh heavens, what must he think of her? She didn't know what to think of herself.

"Sorry for kissing me?"

"I'm confused. Between getting dumped by Jesse and this whole Don Juan thing. I'm just really, really confused right now and I'm taking it out on you. That was wrong of me."

"You didn't do anything wrong."

She plastered a perky smile on her face and glanced at her watch. "Will you look at the time? It's getting late and we've had enough excitement for one evening. What say we call it a night?"

"Meggie..." He reached out for her, but she danced away. She couldn't bear the words if he said something sweet simply to make her feel better for acting like an oversexed doxy.

"Don't worry, Caleb. Believe me, that kiss meant nothing to me, absolutely nothing."

"Nothing?"

"I've forgotten it already. Honest." She waved a hand as if she kissed men atop the Space Needle every single day of her life.

"And I suppose you want me to forget all about it, too."

"If you don't mind."

"Maybe I do mind."

"Caleb, please," she begged. "I had too much wine. That's all there is to it."

He stared at her a long moment without saying anything. He looked at her with great blue eyes gone dark in the mist. His expression made her heart lock. She felt as if she had crossed some unbreachable boundary and could never make it right, no matter what she said.

A group of rowdy revelers came up to the deck from the restaurant below, thankfully interrupting the awkward silence between them.

"I'm ready to go."

A strange mix of sadness, shame and guilt dissolved into a muddle as thick as the gathering fog. This unfortunate episode was going to not only keep her awake at night, but also cause her to flinch at the memory. She wished the damned fog would enshroud her so totally that she disappeared.

How could she have been so stupid?

In that moment, guilt, sadness and shame morphed into a stinging sense of regret. Despite that Caleb had taken her elbow to steady her on the steps, Meggie felt utterly and completely alone.

The trip to her car was heavy, weighted with a sludge of unvoiced emotion neither of them wanted to explore. After she'd unlocked the vehicle, Caleb opened the driver's door for her. She plunked down in the front seat and looked up, beseeching him with her eyes to forgive her.

"Aren't you getting in?" she asked, when he just kept standing there.

"I think I'll walk. My hotel is only a few blocks." He inclined his head east.

Tears pressed against her eyes. He didn't even want to be in the same car with her. Oh God, had she ruined everything between them? Was their friendship kaput?

"It's chilly and damp."

"I'll be all right."

She should have shut up right there and let it go, but, no, in a wretched attempt to ease her pathetic suffering, she had to push.

"Are we on for tomorrow night? I can get tickets to thc Sonics game."

He shook his head. "I'm booked tomorrow night."

"How about Wednesday?"

"No can do."

Hey, idiot, buy a clue. He doesn't want to see you.

"Saturday? We could hit the aquarium. Go on a harbor cruise."

"I'm going to be pretty busy for the next couple of weeks."

"Oh."

He reached out a hand, trailed a finger down her

cheek. His touch ignited her skin. "It's not what you think."

"You're not looking to avoid me?"

"Of course not."

"Then..." She paused as a new thought popped into her head. "Oh. You've met someone."

"Something like that." His smile softened the edges of his eyes. "She's a very special lady."

How could Meggie have been so self-centered? Her kiss hadn't freaked him out in the way she'd supposed. Caleb had met someone else, and here she'd been thinking he was disgusted by her kiss. What a ninny.

"Why, that's great," she babbled. "Fabulous. I'm so happy for you."

"You are?"

"Absolutely. Sure."

"What about that kiss on the observation deck?"

"I told you, it meant nothing. Go. Enjoy your new girlfriend. You have my blessings."

13

HE CAME TO HER in a dream. Dressed entirely in black. Gone was the flowing white shirt, replaced with a black leather vest and nothing else.

Just leather and bare skin.

But was this a dream? Meggie wondered, her entire body trembling in his overwhelming presence. Or a reality she was afraid to admit? From the moment she'd met him, she'd been caught up in this seductive fantasy where reality and dream merged into something powerfully erotic.

He stared at her, his steely blue eyes enigmatic as always behind that mask. His jaw tightened when he noticed she wore only a gauzy red gown.

Her fingers curled with a savage urge to explore that masculine chin. She ached to press her tongue against it, to taste the saltiness of his skin.

He reached for her. When his rough fingers grazed her wrist, she hissed as if burned. His firm clasp propelled liquid heat to the soft tender flesh between her legs.

His expression was unreadable. He did not smile. He pulled her to him and captured her lips with a kiss so tempestuous it took her breath.

He drove the spear of his tongue deep inside her mouth. The taste of him filled her. His mustache grazed her upper lip with a light tickle that launched a languid shiver down her spine.

Her skin hummed with severe pleasure. Her nipples tightened.

He made a hungry male animal noise and ground his pelvis against hers. Their bodies fit perfectly. Streamers of fiery heat flowed from him to her.

Oh, this felt so good.

She breathed hard against his mouth, taking in the scent of man and leather and sex.

"Don Juan," she whimpered.

"Yes, yes?"

"I want you inside me. I want you now."

He pushed her back onto the bed, pressing her body into the mattress. He stripped off his vest, his pants, and settled his weight over her body. With brazen fingers, he ripped the material of her nightgown, exposing her nakedness.

This was what she missed. What she wanted. His forcefulness, his boldness, his daring.

"Hurry, please hurry," she begged. "I'm wet and ready."

He drove into her. Hard, hot, powerful. Again and again and again. She felt as if all the air had been knocked from her lungs.

And then they came in one blistering moment, crying together in rough, desperate groans.

He collapsed upon her, drenched in sweat and love juices.

Slowly, slowly, they drifted back down to earth.

"Let me see your face," she whispered a few minutes later. "I must know who you are."

"How long I've waited for you to say that."

Then he raised his head, peeled off his mask along with the false mustache, unveiling himself to her.

Oh God! What had she done?

Her masked lover was Caleb!

That's when she cried out and jerked herself awake.

Meggie bolted upright in bed, her heart pounding, her body soaked in perspiration, her covers flung to the floor. The dream seemed so real. Too real. She splayed a hand over her chest.

On trembling legs she went to the bathroom and took a shower to cool her scorched skin.

Why had she dreamed Caleb was Don Juan? Fretfully, she dried her body, which strangely enough was as tender as if she actually had made love with him.

Mind in turmoil, she padded to the kitchen and poured herself a glass of tomato juice. She sat at the table and tried to decipher her dream.

Subconsciously, did she want Caleb to be Don Juan?

Meggie gnawed her bottom lip. The two men were different as night and day, even though upon reflection they did possessed similar physical characteristics. Both were tall and lean, dark-haired and blue-eyed.

But Don Juan was wickedly naughty, intrepid and brash, definitely not the sort of man you married. Caleb was sweet and kind and caring, the kind of guy you'd love to bring home to Mother. Too bad Meggie couldn't have both. The exciting lover who revved her blood and made her dare, mixed with the steady, reliable man she could always count on.

And then she had her answer. No wonder she'd dreamed that Caleb was Don Juan. She was attracted to both of them, but she had reservations about each. Caleb was too quiet, too familiar; Don Juan too wild, too reckless. Her subconscious had simply taken the two and melded them into one.

The perfect man who didn't exist.

"YOU ARE THE MOST naturally gifted dancer I have ever had the privilege to instruct," Luisa Roman told Caleb two weeks and ten salsa lessons later. "And such a determined student. I have never seen anyone pick up the tango with such ease."

"Thank you." He accepted the certification of completion she handed him.

His instructor didn't know the half of it. Over the past fourteen days, when Caleb hadn't been either giving lectures at local hospitals or attending classes here at the dance studio, he'd been in his hotel room practicing the elegant yet seductive moves.

Last week, he'd almost run into Meggie in the hallway at the studio as she came out of her belly dancing class, but he'd spotted her first and, just in the nick of time, dashed into the men's locker room. Even though it was a little cruel, he would rather have her thinking he was out with another woman than uncover his plan before he was ready.

But time was not on his side. He was leaving Seattle the following Tuesday. He had to act quickly. He was determined to impress Meggie and he intended to do it up right. Make a grand romantic gesture. Give her one thrilling night she would remember for the rest of her life.

A night they would never forget.

He was ready to push all boundaries, risk everything in order to win her over. Take a chance and grab for the brass ring. He was going to prove to her that their kiss at the top of the Space Needle had indeed meant something very special.

The lessons were finished, he'd even impressed Luisa Roman, and now he was ready.

Even though it had been pure torture, he'd resisted calling Meggie these past two weeks. He wanted her to think about him. To remember their kiss. To wonder what it meant. Yes, he was playing a mind game with her, but then he was counting on a huge payoff.

Love.

Did he have the courage to seduce her without the Don Juan mask? He would find out for certain on Saturday night, when he took her salsa dancing. He imagined the moment and his heart swelled with possibilities.

Then Luisa Roman said something that altered the trajectory of his plans. "Because you are my prize student, I will tell you of a very special place."

"Ma'am?"

She pressed a card into his palm. He glanced at the bold black lettering that said simply The Mystery Room, with an address underneath.

"The Mystery Room?" He raised an eyebrow.

"An exclusive nightclub, offering the finest in salsa dancing and a little more." Luisa's voice had gone low, suggestive.

"A little more?"

"The patrons attend in costume and masks. No bare faces allowed."

Just the thought sent a thrill rippling through his body, and Caleb knew then that he would pose as Don Juan one last time to lure Meggie to the Mystery Room.

"It is very erotic," Luisa continued. "And if you have a special lady, you might want to rent one of the rooms above the club. It's amazing what a night of mystery will do for your love life."

"No kidding."

Perfect. The pieces of his plan fit like a puzzle. He would invite Meggie to the club and dance with her all night. Afterward he would take her upstairs, make love to her and then remove his mask.

"*HELL-OOO.* Meggie, are you even listening to me?" Wendy's voice broke through her reverie.

"Huh?"

"I asked you twice if you thought I should shave my head and you never even blinked, much less offered an opinion. You're a gazillion miles away. What's the matter? Still mooning over that foreign guy?"

Meggie shook her head. They were in her apartment, measuring for new living room curtains. She'd decided she needed a change, but she couldn't seem to force herself to concentrate on the task at hand.

No, she wasn't mooning over Don Juan. She was thinking about Caleb. Worrying about him, actually. He was a babe in the woods when it came to city living, and she wondered about the woman he was seeing. What if she was just some gold digger looking to get at his money? What if the wench ended up breaking the poor guy's heart? Meggie gritted her teeth. If that happened, she would personally hunt the twit down and crack her skull.

The vehemence of her thoughts startled Meggie.

"Oops, there you went again. One minute you're looking me in the eye, the next minute staring off into space," Wendy said. "What gives?"

"Nothing. I'm sorry. I called you over to help me and then I get distracted on you."

"Hey, what are friends for, except to be there when you need them?"

Caleb was her friend.

Or at least he used to be.

God, why had she kissed him? Meggie cringed and dropped her face in her hands. Had she ruined their friendship for good?

She'd been agonizing over that stupid kiss for the past two weeks, wondering why Caleb hadn't phoned, but too embarrassed to pick up the phone and call him. And she'd even been too ashamed of herself to confess to Wendy what she'd done, or talk about that crazy dream where she'd wished Caleb was sexy Don Juan.

"I'm not sure, though, that I've completely forgiven you for not introducing me to your handsome Alaskan naturalist before some hussy scooped him up." Wendy pretended to pout.

"Sorry." Meggie felt a twinge of guilt and regret. If she hadn't been so selfish, if she'd introduced Caleb to Wendy, he probably wouldn't have met that other woman at all, whoever she might be. At least if he'd been with Wendy Meggie would have had a chance to see him.

The telephone jangled.

Caleb? Her hopes soared as they did every time the

phone rang. But this time, for some reason, she had an overwhelming sense it was him.

She raced across the living room, stumbling over the coffee table and whacking her shin.

Ow, ow, ow.

But even pain didn't slow her down.

"'Lo," she answered, her pulse pounding wildly.

"Belladonna."

"Don Juan," she whispered.

In a second Wendy popped in front of her, eyes wide, a huge grin on her face. Meggie waved her away, her mind spinning with a thousand splintered thoughts. Just when she thought she'd put Don Juan in her past where he belonged, here he was again.

"You sound disappointed," he accused in that rich Spanish accent.

"Oh, no. I'm not disappointed. I was just expecting someone else."

"Ah. Another lover?"

"No, no. A friend."

"I have missed you," he crooned, and she felt that old helplessness weaken her knees.

"I never expected you to call me again."

"And why is that?"

"The way you left me the last time we were together, I assumed it was a one-time thing."

"Never assume. Life is too full of surprises for that."

"Are you back in Seattle on business?" she asked, unable to identify the emotions churning inside her, not knowing if she wanted him to be here or not.

"Yes. And I wish to see you again."

A shivery thrill leaped through her. *Oh no. Here we go again.*

"Are you still there?"

Meggie hesitated. "I'm still here."

"Are you busy Saturday night?"

This is a really bad idea, Meggie. Say no.

Ah, but how she wanted to see him again. She ached to run her fingers through his hair, to be kissed and caressed by him. Don Juan had given her sexual healing. Their arrangement was perfect. Not like this oddness she felt for Caleb. No personal information. No entanglements. No falling head over heels in love. No getting hurt.

And yet she fully understood that this thing with her masked fantasy man was dangerous. She was taking a big chance, walking a tenuous tightrope between just sex and something more. It was too easy to confuse love and sex.

Except that wasn't really true. Sex was pretty cut and dried. It was the excitement that confused her. The titillation. The sexual adventure that promised much more than it could ever deliver on an emotional level.

If she had one more fling with Don Juan, for the sake of her own mental health she had to keep one thing firmly planted in the forefront of her mind. *It's just a little sex. Nothing more.*

"I'm free on Saturday night," she said, dismayed at her own weakness, but riddled with lust at the thought of seeing him again.

"That is very good. You make me so happy. Now, I have a favor to ask of you."

"All right."

"I am sending over a costume. Wear it. Inside the box you will find an address for a nightclub. Meet me there. Eight o'clock on Saturday night. I will be waiting for you," he whispered, and then gently hung up.

THE MYSTERY ROOM, a dark, cozy nightclub filled with people in a variety of exotic costumes, oozed sensuality. The huge salsa band played the lambada and there was some pretty steamy stuff happening on the dance floor.

Caleb checked his watch: 8:05.

His heart hammered and he willed Meggie to appear in the doorway. He had positioned himself with his back to the far wall so he would know the minute she stepped over the threshold.

What if she didn't show? What then?

Caleb bit down on his thumbnail. She simply had to come. His need for her was all-consuming, and so intense he didn't think he could stand the disappointment if she never arrived.

And in that dread-filled moment, she appeared.

She looked breathtakingly beautiful in the red-and-black flamenco outfit he'd had delivered to apartment. Her hair was swept off her neck and decorated with a mantilla, and she wore the black leather mask he had included in the box.

Moisture sprang into his mouth and his stomach clamped tight. In that moment, he knew. He wanted to have children with her. And grandchildren. He wanted to be with Meggie Scofield for the rest of his life.

He should have seen it coming. Should have known

this infatuation with her was much more than physical. He had tried to use sex as a release from his distracting fantasies. Instead of freeing him, however, making love with her had only dug him in deeper.

Without her, he was lost.

She appeared bewildered, sliding her gaze around the club, taking in the band's accomplished horn section, the clutch of colorful dancers writhing on the dance floor, the intoxicatingly exotic lighting. As Caleb stalked toward her, she nervously reached up a hand to pat her hair, making sure her mantilla was staying in place.

When she spotted him, her mouth curled up in a smile of relief, and he found himself grinning like some fool in love. She wet her lips with the tip of her tongue, and when he reached out to take her elbow in his palm, he noticed a telltale pink flush spread up her neck, and her swift intake of breath.

"You came," he exclaimed, and leaned in close to brush his mouth over hers in greeting.

He'd meant the kiss to be light, a hint of welcome, of what was to come. But the minute his flesh touch hers, it was seared. Not to taste her would have been a sin of the highest order, and apparently Meggie agreed because she returned his kiss with a ferocity that rocked him to the soles of his boots.

He thought of the rented room upstairs and his body temperature notched upward. His impulse was to scoop her into his arms, carry her up to the room and get her naked as quickly as possible.

With a great internal struggle, he denied the impulse. He was going to seduce her tonight as no man had ever seduced her, and when his mask was removed and she learned his true identity, she would not be able to deny her real feelings for him.

He would seduce her not only with the dance of love, but with all his heart and soul. Caleb was ready to lay everything on the line and take the greatest risk of his life.

"I almost didn't come," she confessed. "But I can never resist the opportunity to dance."

"Or play games?"

"Or play games." She smiled.

"Then we shall dance, belladonna. And play. Until dawn if you desire."

He signaled the band with a coded message he had worked out with them earlier. It had cost him a handsome tip, but the cue was worth it. Smoothly, the band segued from the mambo into the tango.

Caleb bowed low from the waist and offered Meggie his hand with a courtly flourish. The color riding her cheeks deepened, but she readily accepted his arm and he guided her proudly out onto the dance floor.

The hauntingly dramatic music swept over them with its hypnotic rhythm. Images of all the romantic movies he had ever seen featuring the tango swept through his head. Caleb let himself go, giving over completely to the dance, caught up in the moment when fantasy and reality merged into an idyllic blur.

Meggie inclined her head and gave him a coy smile. "You're an excellent dancer, Don Juan."

"We have only just begun."

At his inscrutable words, Meggie felt her self-control slip even future. The man knew how to charm. She shouldn't have come, but now that she was here, she was glad she had ignored the common sense that had dictated her life up until the moment she'd met Don Juan. She gave herself over to the craziness.

Living *la vida loca.*

She danced with Don Juan as she had never danced with another man. They moved in perfect unison, their bodies pressed close together, stepping in tandem with a smooth fluidity.

A heated calm seeped through her body, replacing her earlier nervousness. She experienced a blissful sense of homecoming, a wondrous peace unlike anything she'd ever known. Her confusion and doubts about coming here vanished as surely as darkness at dawn.

In that single fragment of time, she understood the mystery of creation, recognized the cosmic connection between herself and Don Juan. They were one soul, one entity, even more surely than when they'd made love. His eyes remained locked on hers and she could not look away. Nor did she want to.

Step, step, step, step. They tangoed, never missing a beat.

Everyone else had left the dance floor. The other dancers stood on the sidelines, watching in admiration. Meggie barely noticed their audience. All she focused on was Don Juan, as the scent of his sexy body dominated her senses. It seemed so utterly natural to be encircled in his arms. Even more natural to press her cheek against his and close her eyes.

Time ticked by. She heard the throb of his heart and, overlaying that, the mesmerizing tango beat.

The music and his heartbeat became one sound, strumming with a growing intensity that encompassed her mind, body and soul. The sensation leaped beyond surreal and bordered on budding rapture.

And when he dipped her, she felt her brain short-circuit. She wanted him. No matter how foolish, how stupid, how irrational it might be to sleep with this man again—especially since she was also having sensual feelings for Caleb—she simply could not resist. She had to have Don Juan one last time before she could relinquish her obsession and move on with her life.

They danced for what seemed like hours as one spicy salsa song flowed smoothly into another. From Gloria Estefan's rousing rendition of the conga to the exuberant cha-cha-cha to the sensuously flirtatious rumba, their bodies brushed, touched, seared. Their clothes grew damp with passion and perspiration.

Not once did they take their eyes off each other. Their faces were hidden by the masks, but their souls…through the simmering heat of their melded pupils, they laid their souls bare to each other.

Throb, throb, throb.

The relentless beat pushed them higher and higher. Drums, saxophone, trumpet, keyboard. The instruments bloomed, a musical bouquet of sensual sound.

Their passion for each other escalated with each step they took, drawing them deeper and deeper into a vortex of sexual hunger.

When Meggie swirled, her skirt eddied about her legs in a wild, compelling flash of red satin and black lace. She felt the material slap at her shins, the back of her legs, saw frank desire in the eyes of the other men lining the dance floor.

She felt incredibly beautiful, and for that lofty feeling she could never repay Don Juan. He was such a splendid partner, an utterly charming companion. And she knew he made her look like a much better dancer than she was.

With him, dancing seemed effortless, magical. On and on they danced, until the band played the tango once more. As Meggie kept gazing past his mask and into those blue eyes filled with the promise to give her a night to remember, she knew she would never forget the Mystery Room, the tango or him.

When the song ended, she stopped dancing and splayed her palm over his chest. "I simply must have some water."

"But of course."

He guided her to a table at the back of the club; several of the masked and costumed patrons complimented their dancing skills as they went past.

"I will be right back," he whispered, low in her ear, and then departed for the bar.

Tilting her head, Meggie admired the swagger of his leather-clad hips as he walked away. The man had it going on. No doubt about it. His butt was even cuter than Caleb's, who definitely possessed one primo heinie.

Immediately, Meggie felt disloyal to her old friend. She shouldn't compare Caleb to Don Juan. It was like comparing Granny Smiths to Clementines. Caleb was Caleb and Don Juan was Don Juan. Complete opposites in temperament and comportment.

She wondered for a moment who Don Juan really was, but then quickly squelched the thought. She didn't want to know. Didn't want to unearth something better left buried.

Don Juan returned a few minutes later with two tall glasses of iced water. He sat beside her and took a long drink from his glass. Meggie watched him swallow and realized she was in deep when she found even that simple action incredibly stimulating.

The delicate material of his white, puffy-sleeved shirt clung damply to his masculine chest, and Meggie felt her insides slowly unravel.

His face was flushed from the heat of dancing, and a droplet of water glinted on his lower lip. She wanted to lean over and lick it off, watch the flicker of sexual arousal leap to life in his eyes.

When she realized that, without even trying, he equally mesmerized the women seated at the next table, Meggie had to curl her fingers into her palms to keep from getting jealous. Good thing he was only her temporary lover and not her boyfriend. She would have a hard time dealing with this kind of feminine adoration on a regular basis, especially since Don Juan was such a powerful flirt.

Loyalty is something you would never have to worry about with Caleb, a tiny voice whispered in the back of her mind. Now there is a one-woman man.

Meggie pushed the thought away. She still wasn't ready to deal with her budding feelings for Caleb. Those emotions scared her too much, because she knew he was a man she could actually build a life with.

But Caleb had another woman, and he'd been avoiding her with a fierce diligence ever since she'd kissed him atop the Space Needle. She sighed. She had certainly made a mess of that.

You can't expect all risks to pay off.

The most she could hope for was self-discovery, and she'd certainly found that.

Don Juan placed his hand over hers. The familiar jolt of electricity shot through her. She raised her head and met his stare.

"Is something wrong?"

"No."

"You seem unhappy. Is it me?"

"Not at all."

She smiled, trying hard to dispel the sad wisp of longing in her heart. She wasn't right for Caleb and she knew it. She was older than him. She had a life here in the city. He needed a woman his own age or younger, an earthy type who would embrace life in the wilderness.

Don Juan lifted her hand to his mouth and slowly began kissing each knuckle and then running his tongue over her skin until her fingers tingled with the fire of his masculine heat.

If Caleb could see her now, would he be shocked by her indiscretions?

Probably.

What was happening to her? Why did she keep thinking about Caleb when she was in this exotic club with a dashingly charismatic man who impressed her with his flashy dance moves? She was very confused and she knew it. But this was the last time she would see Don Juan. She'd best make the most of their final encounter.

"This club is also an inn," he murmured, low and husky, in his devastating accent. "And I have reserved us a room. Would you like to go upstairs with me now?"

14

HE LED HER UP the narrow staircase illuminated only by wall scones holding red bulbs. When they reached their room on the second floor, Don Juan did not turn on the lamp, but the curtain was open and a soft glow from the streetlights fell across a four-poster, king-size bed with a leather upholstered headboard.

Closing the door behind them with a soft click, he pulled her into his arms and ran the tip of his tongue over her lips, gently probing the warm recesses of her mouth.

She caught his head in her palms and sank her fingers in his raven hair. She melted into his arms, offering herself to him and giving without restraint.

A deep, guttural sound of pleasure slipped from his throat, a hungry, greedy noise that raised the hairs on her arms and filled her with a deep sexual need.

This might be wrong, but heaven help her, nothing had ever felt so right.

"What game are we playing tonight?" he asked. "The choice is yours."

What game indeed?

He understood her need for fantasy. Her mind hopped from one scenario to another. Since this was absolutely the last time she was going to be with him,

Meggie craved a thrill to remember—a provocative memory she could carry with her to the grave.

Her mind snagged on one idea, and when the mere thought of it caused her knees to weaken and her pulse to grow thready, she knew what she wanted.

"I want you to tell me what to do," she whispered, trembling with excitement as the new sex game unfurled in her brain.

"You want me to command you to do things to me?"

Yes. She wanted him to be in control. She needed to relinquish the reins, allow him to lead her to a place of sexual discovery where she had never dared enter.

"Tonight, I am your slave. You are my master. I must do whatever you tell me."

"Are you sure? This is a perilous game, indeed."

Meggie shivered and whispered, "I know. That's why I want it."

"You are a goddess," he murmured.

"No. I am a slave. I am here to do your bidding. What is your pleasure, master?"

"If you are certain."

"I am."

"Take off your clothes." His voice changed, grew rough, dark and demanding. The shift in him both thrilled and scared her.

With shaky hands, Meggie slowly removed her clothing.

Don Juan sat in a wooden, hard-backed chair positioned in front of the window. He said not a word, but watched her with a hard-edged gaze.

She kicked off her high-heeled shoes and fumbled

with the buttons on her dress, her hands perspiring so much her fingers kept slipping.

When she was finally down to her black lace bra and thong panties, Meggie discovered she was reluctant to go further—whether from nervousness or a desire to prolong the game, she couldn't say. Probably a bit of both.

Don Juan was massively aroused, a fact his tight-fitting leather pants made clearly evident. He suddenly seemed very dangerous, and she didn't know what to expect. After all, she didn't really know the guy, had no idea what he was capable of, even though they had intimately explored each other's bodies.

She crossed her arms over her chest and cowered.

"Come here."

Meggie hesitated.

"Come here, slave. Don't make me repeat myself or there will be dire consequences."

He stared at her with such arrogant disregard, his haughty eyes enshrouded by that mask, that Meggie almost stopped the game by crying out, "Enough." But at the same time she was panicking, she felt the crotch of her panties growing decidedly moist.

"Now!"

Tentatively she inched across the room to where he sat enthroned on his chair.

"On your knees."

Slowly she slid to the floor, her pulse jackhammering in her head. Ribbons of sensation streamed through her when she saw just how turned on he was. She licked her lips.

"Now untie my pants."

No sweet croons of "belladonna." No soft mur-

murs, no tender touches. But she had asked for this and her body was swamped with a degree of stimulation she'd never before reached. The thick wetness in her panties seeped down her thighs.

She untied his pants and tipped her head upward to study his face. His jaw was stiff and uncompromising. Pale lines of strain bracketed his mouth. The mask covered half his face, hiding much of his emotion.

What kind of man lurked beyond that facade?

He reached out and grazed her chin with the rough pad of his thumb. "Do I excite you, slave?"

"Yes, master. I am wet for you."

"Pull down your panties and let me see."

She hooked her thumb beneath the waistband of her panties and self-consciously edged them over her hips and down her thighs.

"Straddle me."

Trembling, she did as he commanded, placing one leg on either side of his thigh and resting her bare bottom against his leather pants. With a forefinger, he stroked between her legs, brusquely caressing her heated wetness.

Meggie tossed her head at the abruptness of the experience. His fingers curled inside her and she almost came right then and there.

"Do you want it rough?"

"You are the master. I am the slave. My only wish is to please you."

"Then kiss me."

His breath flew from his body in a smothered rush of sound as her mouth covered his. She tasted his hunger, felt his desperation. The kiss claimed them both, a whirlwind feeding on its own power.

The next moments passed in a desperate flurry as Don Juan lifted her from him, stripped off his clothes, sat back down and pulled her backward, into his lap. For the first time she realized he could see their reflection in the mirror running the length of one wall.

A fresh thrill shot through her.

His nipples were adjacent to her shoulder blades; she felt their sharp peaks jutting against her skin.

"Lean back," he demanded. "Let me play with you."

Meggie leaned back against his chest and he ran a hand up to cup her bare bottom in his palm. The sensations he aroused in her were so unbelievably exquisite that tears stung her eyes.

God, this felt so good. Magical.

While one hand kneaded her fanny, the other trailed to her bare breasts. He swept her nipples and pinched them lightly between his fingers, massaging them with the electricity of his masculine body heat. The sensation was at once delicious, sinful and sweetly familiar, like a favorite dessert eaten for the first time after a long hunger strike.

She'd missed his touch so very much. But how was that possible? She'd only been with him twice, and barely even knew him.

Meggie's body grew heavier, more languorous, until it seemed to liquefy into his. He forsook her nipples and returned to making those idle circles around her breasts, until once more he was back, pulling and plucking the straining peaks.

She writhed against him.

He circled back around her breasts.

This time she moaned through clenched teeth when he reached her nipples at last and rolled them between his rough fingers.

Her breath came out in low episodic gasps and her entire body felt swollen and achy with intense arousal. Nibbling her ear, he lifted her higher up on his thighs, her back still pressed to his chest. She felt her moisture slicken his skin.

His lips tugged on her ear. She delighted in the sensation as he began to suck on her flesh and the opal stud nestled in her lobe. She shuddered at the wetness of his tongue, the heat of his mouth.

He spread his legs and, in the process, pried hers farther apart. One hand slid down her breast and across her inner thigh. His other hand continued to gently massage her butt.

At first, she didn't realize what he was doing as he rotated both of them, spreading her thighs wider, moving closer to the mirror. And then she caught a glimpse of their reflection, the tantalizing picture of his naked flesh pressed against hers.

She gasped, scandalized, embarrassed and monumentally turned on.

She had never made love in front of a mirror. It seemed a wickedly sinful thing to do. She closed her eyes and turned her head.

His devilish laugh rang in her ears. ''Look at yourself. Watch me make love to you.''

And, heaven help her, watch she did.

He bent her over the dresser and she clung to the furniture for dear life, her entire body trembling. He lightly smacked her bottom.

‘‘What an ass.’’ He clutched her butt with both hands and sighed rhapsodically, as if having an oversize caboose was something to be proud of.

Their bodies shifted in the throes of pleasure. Sometimes she could see more of him, sometimes more of herself. The picture in the mirror was a hundred times more erotic than any dirty movie ever filmed. She lost all sense of herself, all sense of time and place.

The world tumbled, an easy glide into ecstasy. When she was quivering and oh so wet, he paused long enough to slip on a condom. He spent a few moments working her up again and then finally, *finally,* he slowly entered her from behind. She whimpered like a grateful puppy.

‘‘You are so beautiful,’’ he murmured, and sweetly stroked her hair.

His gentle croon, his loving caress, fueled her fervor. She tried to move, to give as good as she was getting, but he wouldn’t allow it.

‘‘No,’’ he whispered, and held her still by tugging lightly on her hair. ‘‘If you do that, I won’t last a moment.’’

With much difficulty, she restrained herself. And each time she was about to shoot over the edge, he shifted his body just enough so it didn’t happen.

Frustration welled in her throat. ‘‘Please,’’ she begged. ‘‘Please.’’

‘‘What do you want?’’ he whispered roughly, pushing deeper into her. ‘‘Tell me. What do you need?’’

‘‘Please.’’ She choked on the word, barely able to speak at all.

‘‘More? Do you want more?’’

"Yes...oh yes."

His tone was gruff and tender and thick with the same emotion that clogged her throat. "Not yet, sweetheart. Not yet."

A long, fat sob spilled from her lips as he lifted her off him. She tried to turn, to take hold of him and force him to finish what he had started, but he had stepped back.

She could see him in the mirror; the light from the street glinting in through the blinds cast him in silhouette. She saw the hard, broad thrust of his erection. Blindly she reached for him.

He caught her wrist before she could make contact. "Wait. Please. Just a little bit longer. It will be worth it, I promise."

Then he bent, scooped her into his arms and carried her to the bed. He settled her on the covers and then stepped back. Meggie peered at him. She watched him illuminated in the light from the streetlamp outside the window, his face cloaked by the mask. If she reached out, she could easily flick that cover up and stare straight into his eyes.

"Take off my mask," he demanded. "I want you to see my face."

"No," she whispered, her pulse suddenly pounding so much she feared she might have a heart attack on the spot.

"I am your master and you are my slave. You must obey me."

"I won't."

"Then I must punish you."

"Go ahead."

Don Juan pinned her to the bed. "Take off my mask, slave."

She was on the verge of hysteria. She could not, would not, remove his mask. Her mind balked at the very idea. She did not want to know who he was. It would ruin everything, and she feared he was leading up to more than an unmasking. She worried that he was falling in love with her. She simply could not have that happening.

Meggie realized then she needed the fantasy of the unobtainable male. His games had sustained her, bolstered her self-esteem and renewed her belief in her womanhood after her divorce.

But the last thing she needed in her life was another bad boy. She'd made that mistake once. She wasn't about to do it again. Fireworks might be nice for a fantasy, but real life commitment required so much more than spice and flash. What she needed was an emotionally secure guy. A quiet, steady man. Like Caleb.

Except Caleb already had another woman.

"Take off my mask," he repeated.

"No! Enough! I won't."

"Why not?" he growled.

"Because I don't want to know who you are. Don't you get it? I don't want to see your face. I don't want to fall in love with you. I need security. I need a man who can provide for me, not some gadabout pretty boy who likes to dress up and play sex games with strangers!"

MEGGIE'S WORDS SHATTERED Caleb's world.

She wanted a man to provide for her. She didn't

care about love, but security. She was no different from those women who had shown up in Bear Creek seeking to marry him because he was a millionaire.

Disappointment and a great sadness washed over him, but those emotions were quickly replaced by anger.

"Then why are you here with me?"

Meggie blinked up at him, her face obscured by her own mask. "Why, for the sex games, of course."

Sex. She wanted him for sex. He was either a wallet or a sex object.

You're one to talk, Greenleaf. You started this whole mess with the intention of living out your teenage fantasy. No sense blaming her for something that's your fault. She told you from the beginning she wasn't looking for anything serious. You're the one who messed things up.

His conscience scolded him, but his heart was aching so much he didn't want to hear anything rational.

"So it's sex you want?" His voice grated rudely in his own ears.

She nodded. Her eyes widened, looking rather frightened, but also very excited.

"Then sex is what you'll get."

He shouldn't have taken her. He was too mad and he knew it but, dammit, he couldn't help himself. This was the last time he would be intimate with her.

Caleb parted her thighs with his hands, positioned his body over hers, and then in one forceful, barbaric thrust buried himself deep within her warm wetness, in a pathetic attempt to assuage his despair.

"Oh yes!" she exclaimed, wrapping her slender

arms around his neck, arching her hips upward and pulling him deeper inside her. "Yes."

Sensation, hot and solid, spread outward from the core of his belly. He might not be able to love her forever, but he could love her tonight. And she loved him back, in her way, using her hands and her mouth. Caressing him, biting him, tugging impatiently on his hair whenever he slowed.

Nothing mattered now. Not the past. Not the future. There was only this moment.

He shifted, going from long, slow thrusts to short, quick ones.

"Yes," she whimpered, her eyes squeezed tightly shut. "I like that. More. Deeper. Harder. I want you to fill me up. More...give me more."

She hugged him with her love muscles, tightening around him with each thrust and parry. His heart slammed into his chest, into his ears, into his head, swamping his body with a heat so intense he felt as if he were on fire.

He stopped moving and stared down at her.

"What's the matter?"

"Look at me."

She raised her lashes to peer up at him, and he almost stopped breathing at the expression of sweet longing in her eyes. With his gaze fastened on her like a heat-seeking missile locked on a target, he began to move again.

She surrounded him, engulfed him, absorbed him so completely that he couldn't say where he ended and she began. He'd never experienced anything like it. Not with anyone.

It wasn't her sexiness—although she certainly was

sexy! It wasn't simply a testosterone dump. It wasn't the masks or the games or the mystery of the moment. And it wasn't even the notion that he would never have her again after tonight.

Rather it was the yearning in her eyes. The solid connection between them. The sensation that they were the only two people on the face of the earth.

It was too much to take. Particularly since she'd just made it clear she didn't want him for anything more than sex or money. He'd spent his entire life being loved and respected only for what he could provide, never for simply being himself.

The old pain, along with this new one, knotted his chest. It was all too much emotion, too much hurt, to contemplate. He refused to think anymore.

He broke his visual bond with her then. Closing his eyes, shutting himself off, pulling away like he did when feelings got too intense.

Caleb thrust harder, faster. Meggie growled her pleasure, sounding all the world like a she-cat. She ran her nails down his back, scratching him lightly. She wrapped her legs around his waist and clung tight. She lifted her head off the pillow and nibbled on his bottom lip.

"Almost," she cried. "Don't stop."

He was about to make her come and he'd never felt so proud, so manly. Pushing into her one last time, Caleb felt her convulse around him, just as his masculine essence shot from his body in a splurge of release.

In his blind, heady rush of energy, he cried out her name, forgetting that Don Juan was not suppose to know it. Forgetting, in fact, to use his Spanish accent.

He forgot everything except that for the first and last time he and Meggie had shared the ultimate act of intimacy. He had made love to her with all his heart, mind and soul.

And the awful thing was, it hurt more excruciatingly than anything he could ever have imagined.

15

I DID IT. I took a walk on the wild side. I lived a little. I made my own adventure. I had a no-strings-attached affair and proved I'm not a dud in bed.

She'd gotten what she wanted.

Why then did her victory feel so hollow? Why was she aching for something more? And why couldn't she stop wishing that the man in the bed beside her was not this dashing, unobtainable masked stranger, but rather her dear friend and confidant, Caleb Greenleaf?

Kind, sensitive, intelligent, caring Caleb.

She had thought she had wanted mindless, feel-good sex. She had thought that proving Jesse wrong was a worthy objective. Instead, she'd discovered that revenge was never sweet, and while Don Juan had indeed satisfied her most forbidden fantasies, her real craving wasn't for adventuresome sex at all, but for true and lasting intimacy. Something she would never find through meaningless encounters with strangers.

She'd been looking for love in the wrong place, when Caleb had been right under her nose all along.

Could she be in love with Caleb?

No. That was crazy. She'd known him most of her life. If she'd been in love with him wouldn't she have realized it long before now?

Okay, then why did she keep thinking about him? Why, in the middle of having sex with Don Juan, had she kept pretending he was Caleb? Not to mention that weird dream she'd had. And why did she continue to wonder what Caleb would say if he could see her now?

He would be so disappointed that she'd been unable to resist Don Juan's seductive allure. Shame had her swinging her legs over the side of the bed and searching for her clothing in the darkened room.

Don Juan sat up. She refused to look at him.

"So you are going?"

"Yes."

"I will never see you again." It was a statement, not a question. He got up and came toward her.

"No." She shook her head, reached around to zip the back of the flamboyant flamenco dress.

"You have taken from me what you needed."

"Yes." That sounded so cruel, so cold. "You've given me a lot, Don Juan. You've given me back my femininity and I can't thank you enough for that."

"You are welcome." Gently, he touched her cheek. "I will always remember you fondly."

She slipped her feet into her shoes and then turned to go. She hesitated at the door, her hand on the knob. "Take care of yourself, okay?"

"Adios, belladonna," he whispered in the Spanish accent that no longer sent chills of desire pushing down her spine. "Adios."

MEGGIE PACED THE LENGTH of Wendy's kitchen floor, arms crossed over her chest, a thousand conflicting thoughts tumbling through her brain. She'd arrived at her friend's apartment not long after leaving Don Juan's bed, still dressed in her elaborate dancing costume. She'd desperately needed someone to talk to, but now that she was here, she didn't know how to begin.

"Whoa, girlfriend," Wendy said. "You're gonna wear out the linoleum way ahead of its time."

Pace, pace, pace. Hit the wall. Pivot. Pace, pace, pace. Repeat.

She liked the short rhythm of measuring off Wendy's small kitchen in her high-heeled shoes. It kept her focused on something other than her tumultuous feelings.

"Can you at least give me a hint at what's got you so agitated?"

Meggie opened her mouth and started to speak, but then sighed and just shook her head, not knowing how or where to start.

"What? Talk to me. How can I help if you don't tell me what's going on?"

"It's all wrong," Meggie finally said.

"What's all wrong?"

"What I'm feeling."

"You're gonna have to clue me in." Wendy's brow dipped in an expression of concern. "What are you feeling?"

"I think I've fallen in love with him."

Wendy gasped. "Oh, Meggie, I knew you were going to lose your heart. You're just not the kind of girl who can love 'em and leave 'em."

Irritated, Meggie waved a hand. "That's where you're wrong. I used Don Juan to bolster my damaged ego and I thanked him and walked away." She snapped her fingers. "Just like that."

"But I thought you said you thought you were falling in love with him."

She shook her head. "Not Don Juan."

"Then who?"

"Caleb."

"What?" Wendy looked as shocked as Meggie felt.

"I know. It's illogical, irrational, but there it is. I'm in love with him."

"Wow."

"The awful thing is, he doesn't feel the same way about me."

"How do you know?"

"I kissed him," Meggie admitted. "And he backed off. Quick. Told me he'd met someone else."

"Ouch."

Meggie bit her bottom lip to keep from crying. "I feel like such an idiot."

"Are you sure Caleb doesn't have feelings for you? If he just met this woman, surely it's not that serious. What if you told him how you felt?"

"I can't do that," Meggie wailed.

"Why not?"

Why not indeed?

Because she was afraid to put her heart on the line. Afraid of getting hurt again. How did she know that what she was feeling for Caleb was real and not some weird case of transference? But all the signs of real love were there, weren't they? Her heart skipped a beat whenever she heard his name. She'd melted when they'd kissed. She had erotic dreams about him.

He took a risk for you, Meggie. Remember that night atop the Space Needle when he dared to brave those heights? Take a chance on him. He might surprise you.

"You owe it to you both to at least go and talk to him," Wendy said. "Ask yourself this—what have you got to lose if you don't?"

Meggie eyed her friend, swallowed hard and whispered, "Everything."

"I'M SORRY, MA'AM. Mr. Greenleaf has checked out."

"Checked out?" Numbly, Meggie stared at the desk clerk. "What do you mean, checked out?"

"Mr. Greenleaf paid his bill and vacated the premises about..." the man consulted his watch "...an hour ago."

"No. There must be some mistake. He has one more lecture to give. He's not supposed to leave town until the middle of the week."

Even to her own ears her voice sounded high and desperate. The desk clerk probably thought she was a certified nutcase.

The clerk shrugged. "I'm sorry," he repeated.

"Maybe he moved to another hotel. Did he leave a number where he could be reached?" She curled her fingers around the counter and stood on tiptoes to peer over the desk, as if the paperwork stretched out in neat piles might reveal some clue about Caleb's unexpected departure.

"No. He left no forwarding number."

"Oh." Meggie let out a sigh and settled the soles of her shoes back down on the ground. She felt as if she'd just taken a swift kick to the solar plexus. Where had Caleb gone?

Perhaps he's staying with his new girlfriend. The thought hit her like a sledgehammer.

"Wait." The clerk pulled a yellow Post-it off the edge of a nearby computer screen. "Are you Meggie Scofield?"

She pressed a hand to her throat. "Yes. Yes, I am."

"It seems Mr. Greenleaf left a package for you."

"A package? For me?" she parroted.

"Just a minute. I'll get it from the back room."

"Okay."

The clerk disappeared through a door behind the desk. Meggie glanced down at her hands and was surprised to find them trembling.

Calm down. Don't jump to conclusions.

A couple of minutes later the desk clerk returned with a brown paper bag. "Here you are, Ms. Scofield."

Meggie took the sack and went to sit down in a plush upholstered chair in the lobby. She set the sack on the floor, opened it up and removed a pair of shiny, knee-length leather boots.

What the heck?

Her pulse skipped erratically. What was this?

Next she extracted a pair of black leather draw-string pants, a black cape and a white, puffy-sleeved pirate's shirt. By the time she reached the bottom of the bag and the black leather mask, Meggie literally could not breathe.

She stared at the evidence in her hand, at first choosing not to comprehend what it meant. Then she sucked in a shuddering breath.

Oh no! Oh no! It couldn't be!

Don Juan and Caleb, one and the same? Just like in her dream?

Disbelief knifed her belly.

Caleb simply could not be Don Juan. No way. There had to be another explanation. Honest, trustworthy Caleb would never have deceived her this way.

The main question was, why?

Why had this kind, understated man gone to great lengths to hide his real self? Why the charade? Was it because he simply wanted an erotic adventure of his own before finding a wife and settling down for good? Meggie cringed to realize she had been far more than eager to oblige.

Or was there a more deep-seated reason?

Denial is not just a river in Egypt, honey.

Meggie rubbed her fingers over the leather mask and clamped her lips closed over a deep, mournful moan. Her life was filled with lies, lies and more lies. The lies Caleb had told her. The lies she'd told herself.

She had wanted so desperately to believe in a fantasy, to relish the way he made her feel as a sexual being, that she had been too selfish to see beyond the mask to the real man beneath. In an attempt to assuage her emotional pain and bolster her self-confidence, she'd accepted Don Juan at face value. She'd gone seeking shallow pleasures, telling herself it was all in the name of living a little.

She hadn't wanted to look beyond surface appearance. Why else had she insisted they make love in the dark after the Halloween party? Why else had she refused to remove his mask last night, even after he'd begged her to?

That's when she realized the startling truth. Somewhere deep down inside her, in the part that had ached to live out her wildest fantasies, she'd secretly known all along that Don Juan was Caleb. She had wanted the pleasure without accepting the responsibility of a real relationship, so she had willingly indulged in his pretense.

And now they were both in pain. Suffering for their perilous masquerade.

She had no one to blame for this mess but herself.

CALEB SNOWSHOED through the forest. He'd gotten reports of poachers in the area, and he was checking out the sightings, but his heart wasn't in his work. He missed Meggie something fierce. Missed her and hated himself for his weakness.

It had been almost two weeks since he'd left Seattle and returned home to Bear Creek. Two weeks, and he hadn't heard a word from her. He told himself he was glad, that it was for the best. But he was lying.

For the hundred millionth time, he imagined her sitting in the lobby of the Claremont Hotel, looking through the paper bag, realizing for the first time that he was her masked lover.

His gut twisted at the thought of her pain.

She probably despised him. Probably felt pretty darn betrayed.

Well, no more than he. Caleb had thought Meggie was different. That if any woman could accept him for the man he was and not for the money he'd made, Meggie would have been the one. When she'd told him she needed security, she'd as good as turned his soul inside out and stomped on it with both feet.

Yeah? Well, buddy boy, how can you expect her to accept you for your authentic self when you deceived her? Lies don't breed trust.

How many countless times had he had this argument with himself since returning home? A thousand? Ten thousand?

He should let the whole thing go, stop poking and prodding the snafu with his mind. It was better this way. They'd had great sex. Both of them had gotten their needs met. Problem was, he'd romanticized the situation, made out their loving to be more than it was.

So why the hell couldn't he stop thinking about her—and wishing things could be different?

Caleb snorted, disgusted with himself. He'd manufactured this house of cards. He shouldn't have been surprised when it came tumbling down. Solid relationships were built on honesty and trust. They had neither. Because without honesty, how could you trust someone?

He tramped through the forest, not really noticing where he was going. The wind gusted with the waning daylight. He snuggled deeper into his parka and raised his head to see where he was. He should be getting back to the ranger station before nightfall.

That's when he saw where his subconscious had been leading him.

To the clearing in the woods. To the skaters' cabin where he and Meggie had first become intimate. He stared at the cabin, remembering, and a fresh tear rendered his heart in two.

16

THE TELEPHONE RANG.

As she'd been doing for the past three weeks every time the stupid thing jangled, Meggie jumped and made a mad dash for the receiver.

Caleb?

"Hello?"

"Meggie?"

Her hopes fractured. "Kay?"

"What's going on?" her friend demanded in a none-too-pleasant tone of voice. "Your mother just told me that you're not coming home for the holidays."

"I can't afford the time off from work," Meggie said.

It wasn't a total lie. She'd recently been promoted, so there was no problem with her job. Although she was entitled to take time off at Christmas, even after taking a leave of absence this past summer, working overtime during the holidays would go a long way toward earning her additional brownie points with her boss.

But the real reason she'd told her mother she wasn't coming home for Christmas had nothing to do with work and everything to do with Caleb. She wasn't up to facing him again. Not yet. Not now. Not until her heart had plenty of time to heal. Whenever the hell that might be.

"I've got to tell you, Meggie, Sadie is really hurt you're not coming back for their wedding."

In the tumult of her messy love life she'd forgotten all about Jake and Sadie's wedding. "I'm really sorry. Tell Sadie I'll make it up to her."

"If she's lucky a girl only gets married once," Kay chided.

"You're right. I'm a terrible friend. What can I say?"

"Just tell me what in the hell happened between you and Caleb."

"Caleb?" Meggie heard her voice rise an octave. "Who said anything happened between me and Caleb?"

"Oh, come on. The way you two were making goo-goo eyes at each other at the *Metropolitan* party, the way Caleb came home in an utterly black mood, the way he scowls whenever your name is mentioned...I'm not dumb."

Stunned, Meggie blinked. "You knew that Caleb was Don Juan?"

"Well, of course I did."

"Why didn't you say something?"

"Because you and Caleb both needed a grand romantic adventure. I don't know what happened, but you two need to make up. It's as obvious as the noses on your faces you guys were made for each other."

"It is?"

"For a smart woman you can sometimes be pretty dense, sister-in-law mine."

"You don't understand. This thing between me and Caleb is very complicated."

"Whatever. But by behaving like a spoiled brat you're hurting a lot of other people."

"Spoiled brat?" Meggie felt herself growing angry.

"Yes, spoiled brat. Just because you and Caleb aren't speaking to each other doesn't mean the rest of us should have to suffer. Your folks want to see you for the holidays. Sadie and Jake want you at the wedding. And there's something else you're needed for. *Metropolitan* found out Bear Creek's health-care needs are grossly underserved and they're planning on holding a Christmas bachelor action as a fundraiser for a new clinic. They wanted to know if you'd serve as spokeswoman."

"They did?"

"Yes. Caleb's going to be in the auction."

Meggie gripped the receiver tighter. "That's not really an enticement."

"Okay, here it is. My big confession. I need you to come home."

"You?" Meggie laughed. Kay was the most self-contained woman she knew. "Why would you need me?"

There was a pause.

Anxiety gripped Meggie. "Kay? You and Quinn aren't having problems, are you?"

"No. Nothing like that."

"What is it then?"

"I need a nurse to assuage my fears."

"Are you sick?" Alarm swept through her at the thought her sister-in-law might be seriously ill.

''Well, not exactly.''

''What then, exactly?''

''Quinn and I were going to wait for Christmas day to spill the beans, but since you won't be here, I might as well tell you now.''

''For heaven's sake, Kay, tell me what?''

''I'm pregnant.''

''LET'S HEAR IT for bachelor number three,'' Kay spoke into the microphone. ''Put your hands together for the single remaining bachelor from the Bachelors of Bear Creek *Metropolitan* ad. You know him, you love him, our own Caleb Greenleaf.''

Wild applause, catcalls and whistles greeted Kay's announcement. Liam Kilstrom shone the spotlight and played a short refrain of ''Bad Boys'' as Caleb strutted out on stage in tight blue jeans and a red flannel shirt. He looked so handsome Meggie forgot to breathe.

Jitterbug nervous, she stood at the back of room, her heart in her throat, running her hands over her brand-new outfit. Red leather pants, red silk blouse, red cowboy boots. She had arrived a few minutes earlier, slipping through the doors and lurking among the crowd. So far only Mack—who had flown her in from Anchorage—knew she was home.

The Bear Creek community center, gaily decorated with red and green Christmas lights, was packed to the rafters with women of all shapes, ages and sizes, eager to bid on the bachelors and add to the charity coffers for the *Metropolitan* clinic fund.

Meggie's stomach knotted. She chewed her bottom lip. She was willing to spend all her savings if that's what it took to win Caleb away from the next highest bidder.

''Let's start the bidding at a hundred dollars,'' Kay called out. ''Who's willing to fork over a hundred dollars for the pleasure of this man's company?''

Two dozen hands shot up.

Meggie cleared her throat. ''Five hundred dollars.''

''Goodness, ladies, you hear that? Someone is willing to shell out five hundred dollars.'' Kay grinned. ''Do I hear five hundred and ten?''

Most of the women who'd bid earlier dropped out, all but one saucy lady that Meggie recognized as Lizzy Magnuson, a friend of Sadie's. Lizzy had recently moved to Bear Creek from San Francisco.

Boldly, Lizzy waved a hand. ''Six hundred.''

''Seven hundred,'' Meggie exclaimed.

Kay shaded her forehead with her hand. ''Okay, who's Miss Moneybags in the back of the room?''

Meggie moved closer to the stage, pushing through the crowd of women, her eyes on Caleb.

He stared at her, first with shocked surprise. Then a wide grin spread across his face and his eyes crinkled in greeting.

Meggie's heart soared. He was happy to see her!

She kept walking. People shifted, allowing her through.

''Seven-fifty,'' Lizzy challenged.

''Eight hundred.'' Meggie never dropped her gaze from Caleb's.

''Nine hundred.'' Lizzy was damned determined, but Meggie was even more so.

''A thousand dollars.'' She arrived at the edge of the stage.

Caleb took the microphone from Kay and dropped to his knees in front of Meggie. His stare drilled a hole straight through her. "Sold to the lady in red for one thousand dollars."

The crowd went nuts, laughing and talking and cheering.

Caleb tossed the microphone back to Kay, hopped down off the stage, took Meggie by the elbow and swept her out the exit and into the cloakroom.

He spun her around to face him. His intense blue eyes ate her up. "You came home."

"I came home." Now that they were alone, she felt her nervousness return.

"For Christmas? For the wedding?"

"For good."

"What? But you're a city girl. You love Seattle. Why would you move back to Bear Creek?"

"A lot of reasons."

"Yeah?" He arched a quizzical eyebrow.

"Well, *Metropolitan* offered me a job running their clinic."

"Oh they did, did they?" He pulled her into his arms. It felt so good. So right. The minute his chest touched hers everything just fell into place.

"Uh-huh. And Kay's going to need a lot of help with that baby. Did you hear? I'm going to be an aunt."

"You being a nurse will really come in handy." His lips were millimeters from hers. His rich, masculine scent filled her nostrils.

"True."

"So are those the only reasons that you decided to move back?"

"Well," she said, enjoying drawing this out, "there is one other reason."

"And that is?"

"I discovered I don't need the big city for excitement, after all."

"No?"

"Nope."

"If that's the case, then how do you plan on getting your kicks from now on?"

"I was kind of hoping you might help me answer that question."

"Me or Don Juan?"

She bit her lip, dropped her gaze. He cupped her chin in his palms, raised her face and made her look at him.

"Why did you leave me that night, Meggie?" Caleb whispered.

It hurt looking him in the eyes and seeing just how much she had wounded him. "I wasn't ready to face the truth. But then again, I wasn't the only one running away. Why did you flee Seattle? Why did you leave me the sack? Why didn't you tell me face-to-face?"

"I owe you an apology for that. I have no excuse. I was scared to death and that's the honest truth."

"What were you afraid of?"

He swallowed so hard his Adam's apple bobbed. "That you only wanted me for my money."

Meggie shook her head. "Why on earth would you think that?"

"When I tried to get you to take my mask off, to acknowledge who I was, you told me you needed security. I realize I'm apprehensive about money issues, because of the way my mother is, because of my childhood. But I was afraid you could never love me for myself.''

''Caleb, I meant *emotional* security. As exciting as Don Juan was, I needed more. Great sex wasn't enough. I needed a strong, steady, reliable man.''

''You thought the sex was great?''

''You're an amazing lover. An amazing man.''

''Really? You don't mind a guy who'd rather commune with nature than join the rat race in pursuit of the almighty dollar?''

''I don't give a damn about your money. Give it away for all I care.''

''You're serious.''

''As a heart attack.''

Caleb couldn't believe what he was hearing. He reached out with his index finger and pushed an inky curl from her cheek. As he stared into her upturned face, he couldn't recall ever having been moved so deeply by anything.

''I've loved you since I was fourteen years old, Meggie Scofield. But because I believed I never stood a chance with you, I convinced myself the attraction was purely physical.''

She gazed up at him with a quiet acceptance in her eyes that gave him the courage to continue.

''I was a goofy kid who liked hanging out in the woods watching animals. You were older and so sophisticated. I knew you were out of my league and yet I couldn't stop fantasizing about being with you.''

''You fantasized about me?''

''Babe, you have no idea.''

''I never thought I was fantasy-worthy,'' Meggie

admitted. "I mean, my butt is too big for the rest of me and I've got freckles and my face is sort of plain and—"

"Shh." He placed his finger on her lips. "I love your butt. It's perfect. I adore your freckles, and your face is most certainly not *plain.* I know you've got this idea that you're not very pretty, and my stupid stepbrother is partially to blame for your distorted sense of yourself, but I'm sorry to disillusion you, Megs. I think you're gorgeous and I always have."

"Honest?" she whispered.

"I tried to forget you. I had a few flings in college and thought I got you out of my system.

"But I never could seem to connect with anyone. Not with the level of intimacy I craved. And then when you strutted into the costume party in that Klondike Kate costume, I was a goner, even though at the time I had no idea it was you."

"I fell for Don Juan the minute I saw him, too."

"No kidding?"

"No kidding."

"When you whispered your phone number to me and I realized Klondike Kate was you I was totally rattled. After what we'd done in the skaters' cabin..." He shook his head. "I wasn't going to act on the attraction. I tried to pretend it never happened. But then I get this invitation from that committee you were on, asking me to give lectures in Seattle and I'm thinking maybe you had figured out that I was Don Juan and this was your way of asking me to come for you."

"I didn't realize you were Don Juan, at least not consciously," she admitted. "But deep down inside,

I knew. That's why I didn't call. I thought I'd just been using you to get over Jesse. But I couldn't stop thinking about you. And when Kay told me how miserable you were, I knew I had to come home. I had to discover if there was a chance for us. Do we have a chance together, Caleb?''

''Do you really have to ask?''

She smiled. ''I love you, Caleb Greenleaf.''

''You know what, Meggie Scofield?''

''What?''

He pointed above her head. Meggie glanced up, saw she was standing under a sprig of mistletoe.

''I love you, too.''

She said, ''Oh,'' just as his mouth closed over hers and he gave her a thrill to remember.

Forever.

Epilogue

MEGGIE AND CALEB WERE married exactly one year to the day after the masked costume ball where suave Don Juan first clamped eyes on his mysterious Klondike Kate. The ceremony took place in the Tongass National Forest on the front porch of the skaters' cabin. The guest list included the entire town of Bear Creek, Meggie's friends from Seattle and the *Metropolitan* editorial staff, who'd insisted on paying for their reception as the last bachelor joined his buddies in wedded bliss.

From where she sat in the audience, Kay shifted baby Ella on her lap, leaned against Quinn's big, comforting chest and whispered, "I told you they were meant for each other."

He laughed softly. "Who am I to argue with an intuitive woman? You convinced me that I was perfect for you and you were right on the money."

"And don't you ever forget it." Kay regarded him with loving eyes.

"As if I ever could." He draped his arm across his wife's shoulder and pulled her and the baby closer to him.

Quinn gazed over the crowd and met the eyes of his buddy Mack, who was one of Caleb's groomsmen. Mack grinned and mouthed, "Look what you started with that advertisement'' and nodded at his wife, Cammie Jo, who was positioned at the makeshift alter. Cammie Jo wore a chic maternity bridesmaid's dress and an expression of pure joy.

Sadie, Meggie's matron of honor, stood beside Cammie Jo. Sadie studied the blushing bride with a hitch of happiness in her throat. Meggie looked completely adorable in her white wedding gown and that red-feathered mask substituting for a veil. And Caleb was pretty darned handsome in his Don Juan outfit. Although, in Sadie's estimation, no one was as handsome as her husband, Jake.

Sadie snagged Jake's gaze. As Caleb's best man, he was positioned across from her. Sadie tipped the corners of her mouth up in a Mona Lisa smile. Jake winked. Just wait until she told him about the outcome of her recent doctor's visit. It looked as if Bear Creek was in for a real population boom, courtesy of those lusty ex-bachelors.

Sadie's attention was drawn back to the ceremony when Caleb started reciting in a deep, poetic voice the wedding vows he'd written himself.

``Darling, you are my sun, my moon, my stars, my everything. My heart lights up when you walk into a room. You've helped me to change, to grow, to become a better man. I promise to spend the rest of my life showing you exactly how much I love you.'' With shaky fingers Caleb took off Meggie's red-feathered mask and gazed into the sweet face he knew as intimately as his own. ``The removal of our masks symbolizes that we lay bare our souls to each other and place our faith in the greatest power of all—real and unconditional love.''

The audience sighed in unison.

Tears rolled down Meggie's cheek as she gazed deeply into his eyes. Caleb's heart thumped with emotion. To think this wondrous day had come at last.

Sadie handed Meggie a handkerchief and she dabbed the tears away before raising her hand to remove his mask.

"I lay bare my soul to you, Caleb Joshua Greenleaf. From this day forward we are one. I, Megan Marie Scofield, take the..."

As she continued, Caleb was aware of nothing except his beloved bride and their bright future together. Not the crowd, nor the minister, not the majestic mountains surrounding them. He was the luckiest man on earth to have captured the heart of the woman he'd loved for half his life, and he knew it.

"I now pronounce you husband and wife," the minister announced.

Caleb's lips took possession of Meggie's in a kiss so powerful her body hummed with its impact. The crowd cheered when he deepened the kiss.

After a long, rapturous minute, he dragged his mouth from hers, pressed his lips to her ear and whispered, "You know we have an hour before the reception starts, Mrs. Greenleaf."

"What are you suggesting, Mr. Greenleaf?" she whispered back, tantalized by his bold innuendo right here in front of everyone.

When she had set her course for adventure that fateful night she'd followed Don Juan into the woods, she had never guessed she would get everything she'd bargained for and then some. Her body tingled with anticipation for what lay ahead.

Caleb took her hand and led her down the path strewn with rose petals. A saddled horse awaited as their getaway ride. The guests got to their feet and blew bubbles as they walked past.

"A game?" he whispered.

"What kind of game?" she murmured, all the while smiling at the crowd. "Master and slave? Doctor and nurse? The Big Bad Wolf and Little Red Riding Hood?"

"You know my favorite."

"Mountain man and city girl?"

"You got it," he growled.

"In the park ranger's cabin?"

"I was thinking on horseback." He stopped beside the waiting steed.

"Caleb!" She spoke too loudly, then glanced over her shoulder to find that everyone was still watching. She ducked her head and lowered her voice. "Is that even possible?"

"Never know until you try."

His strong hands spanned her waist and he lifted her onto the saddle. The crowd cheered and applauded. Caleb climbed up behind her. He gathered the reins and urged the horse into a trot.

They quickly disappeared into the forest. His back was flush against hers, and even through the lacy material of her wedding dress, she could feel the evidence of his desire pressing hard against her fanny.

He slowed the horse to a walk and wrapped his arms around her. Meggie leaned her head into the curve of his neck and sighed deeply. Her mind expanded with the erotic logistics of making love in the saddle.

Caleb growled low in his throat. "You are the sexiest woman in the world. Do you have any idea what you do to me?"

"Mmm." She turned her head and flicked out her tongue, licking a hot, wet trail along his jaw as she slipped her hands behind her back and undid the string ties on his leather pants.

"What...what are you doing?" he asked in a gravelly voice.

"Following up on your fantasy. If we're clever we might not even have to take our clothes off. Oh, by the way, I forgot to mention I'm not wearing any underwear."

His chuckle was low and seductive. "Neither am I, babe. Neither am I."

"I love playing games with you."

"There's no one else on the face of the earth I want to play games with."

Her nimble fingers separated the leather material at his fly, and Caleb's now-exposed rock-hard shaft burgeoned in her hand, letting her know just how much he wanted her.

"Ah, woman, see what your naughty games do to me?"

Meggie trembled with excitement as the man she loved slid his hands beneath her dress, cupped her bare bottom in his palms and lifted her off the saddle.

As he eased her down over his erection, Meggie hissed in her breath and whispered, "Let the games begin."